W9-AFL-355
Harlequin Presents...

Other titles by

ANNE MATHER

IN HARLEQUIN PRESENTS

ANNE MATHER

beware the beast

Harlequin Books

TORONTO • LONDON • NEW YORK • AMSTERDAM • SYDNEY • WINNIPEG

Harlequin Presents edition published May 1977
ISBN 0-373-70689-8

Original hardcover edition published in 1976
by Mills & Boon Limited

Printed in U.S.A.

CHAPTER ONE

THE summons to the solicitor's office came exactly thirty days after her father's accident.

Charlotte was just getting over the initial shock which her father's death had evoked, just beginning to feel her way back to some semblance of normality, if anything could be normal again after such an experience. How had it happened? she had asked herself again and again. How could her father, an experienced yachtsman, have lost all control like that? No one would ever know, she supposed, shuddering as she recalled her father's bloated body washed up at Sheerness.

People had been kind, of course. Her father's friends, his business acquaintances, all had offered her their sympathy and condolences. After all, she was alone in the world now. Her mother had died eight years ago, and although she and her father had never been really close, she being away at school most of the time, she would miss him terribly.

Gradually, though, she had had to assert some interest in her own position. They had not been rich, but then again, they had by no means been poor, and it had come as a great surprise to her to learn that her father had taken out a huge personal insurance policy only weeks before his death. Naturally, this had aroused some suspicion at the inquest, but her father's solicitors had assured the Coroner that he was not in monetary difficulties. Their house, in a little square near Regent's Park, was worth a small fortune by today's standards, and the small company her father had owned seemed to be doing reasonably well. Mortimer Securities was not a large concern, but its profits were steady. There was no obvious reason why Charles Mortimer should have taken his own life, and so far as Charlotte was aware, that line of inquiry had been terminated.

Nevertheless, to discover that almost overnight she had become virtually an heiress troubled Charlotte, particularly as she had never felt any need for a lot of money. She couldn't imagine why her father should have felt obliged to take out such an insurance, and she didn't quite know what she was going to do with it.

At the time of the accident, she had been working on a part-time basis in a boutique in Knightsbridge. The boutique was owned by the mother of a school friend and as Charlotte had only just left school and was still undecided what to do with her education, she had welcomed the chance to earn some pocket money. She enjoyed the opportunity too of studying clothes at close range, and was considering taking up designing herself. There were always art courses available at college.

But all that seemed distant now, unreal, and she blamed herself bitterly for not giving her father more attention. Perhaps he had been tired, overworked; on reflection she could remember a certain look of strain at times. If only she had not been so wrapped up with thoughts of her proposed career she might have persuaded him not to make that final trip.

And then the summons came, a rather chilly little letter which Charlotte read several times before thrusting it away in her handbag. She imagined her father's solicitors were dismayed at her apparent lack of interest in her inheritance. Perhaps they could see their fat fees dwindling now that Charles Mortimer was no longer around to require their services. Whatever, Charlotte was not too concerned. With the finance company being assessed, and doubts already in her mind that she would go on living in their house in Glebe Square, what did she want with a hundred thousand pounds?

It was with some misgivings that she was shown into Mr. Falstaff's office. These surroundings reminded her too vividly of her early visits there immediately after her father's death, and her mouth felt dry and there was a disturbing burning sensation behind her eyes at the remembrance.

Mr. Falstaff was no Shakespearean hero figure. Small, and slight, with wispy grey hair, he looked most like a clerk out of some Dickensian novel, though his eyes were sharp as they took in Charlotte's attractive appearance. Tall and slender, as she was, the events of the past four weeks had fined down her appearance, and in a simple jeans suit with her dark red hair loose about her shoulders, she looked years younger than the eighteen he knew her to be.

They shook hands, and Mr. Falstaff indicated she should be seated in the leather-seated chair opposite his own. Then, remaining standing, he said: "I'm so glad you could come, Miss Mortimer. The matter was – er – rather urgent."

The telephone rang at that moment, and with a click of his tongue, Mr. Falstaff excused himself to answer it. It gave Charlotte a few moments to compose herself, and she looked determinedly round the office, noticing the tome-lined walls describing law practice from the year dot. Why was it, she wondered, that solicitors' offices always had this air of decrepitude and solemnity? Was it because the reasons that most people came here had to do with death and its complications?

Then she thrust such thoughts aside. How morbid could you get? Her father was dead – she had to accept it. It came to everybody in time. What was it somebody had once said? – the only certain thing in life was death? She shivered.

Mr. Falstaff put down the receiver and turned to her again. "I'm sorry about that, Miss Mortimer," he apologized in his dry crackly voice, as dry and crackly as the tomes on the shelves behind him, "I hope we shan't be disturbed again."

"That's all right." Charlotte shook her head. "You wanted to see me?"

She was hurrying things, but she wanted this over. The old solicitor studied her silently for a few moments, and then he nodded, and subsided into his chair as though his thoughts had driven the strength from him.

"Tell me, Miss Mortimer," he said, fidgeting with his pen. "Have you ever heard of Alex Faulkner?"

Charlotte stared at him. "Alex Faulkner? The name doesn't mean anything to me. Should it?"

"That remains to be seen." The lines on Mr. Falstaff's face deepened. "Your father didn't mention his name to you?"

"No. I've told you, I've never heard of him before." Charlotte spoke impatiently.

"No, no, of course not. But surely – you must have heard of Faulkner International?"

"Faulkner International?" Charlotte shook her head. "I don't think so. Look, what is all this? Why do you want to know whether I know this man?"

"All in good time, Miss Mortimer. You will soon appreciate that I am in a rather – er – difficult position, and I am trying to handle this in the best way I know how."

"Handle what?" Charlotte felt a twinge of unease.

"I'm coming to that, Miss Mortimer." Mr. Falstaff shifted uncomfortably. "You were saying – you don't recollect hearing of Faulkner International. I'm surprised. The name is not unknown. Oil – shipping – casinos – "

"Please, Mr. Falstaff, get to the point."

"Very well. Alex Faulkner was an associate of your father's."

"So were lots of people."

"I appreciate that. But this – relationship was rather different."

"In what way?"

"You must understand, Miss Mortimer, Alex Faulkner does not normally involve himself in the actual running of his companies. He employs directors for that purpose. Indeed, few people know him very well. He is not interested in a jet set kind of existence. In fact, I believe he lives very quietly."

Charlotte sighed. "So? What has this to do with me?"

Mr. Falstaff's lips tightened. "Give me time, Miss Mortimer. You young people are so impatient. It is essential that you should understand the picture." He sighed. "Your grandfather knew his father quite well."

"Did he?" Charlotte was beginning to sound bored.

"Yes. I should tell you at this juncture, Faulkner is not exactly a contemporary of your father's. He is, I suppose, almost forty. Your father was some years older, wasn't he?"

"You know he was."

"Yes. Well, they – your father and Faulkner – met again some years ago. Indeed, they shared an interest in sailing. Your father knew France quite well, didn't he?"

Charlotte nodded. "We used to have a small villa – just a cottage really. Daddy sold it a couple of years ago."

Mr. Falstaff nodded. "And he didn't mention Faulkner to you?"

"Why should he? I was still at school. I didn't know all his business acquaintances."

Mr. Falstaff sighed heavily. "This wasn't altogether a business acquaintanceship." He hesitated. "Miss Mortimer, you were aware of your father's interest in gambling, weren't you?"

Charlotte stiffened. "I don't know what you mean."

"I think you do, Miss Mortimer."

"He played the horses a few times. I knew that."

"That's not what I meant. You didn't know of his interest in cards, for example?"

Charlotte twisted her hands together. "I knew he enjoyed cards, yes. He used to play bridge – "

"Not bridge, Miss Mortimer. Poker!"

Charlotte gasped. "No."

Mr. Falstaff shook his head. "This is so much harder than I had anticipated. Miss Mortimer, your father was a compulsive gambler. He had been so for years."

"No!"

"I'm afraid he was."
Charlotte swallowed hard. "Wh-what has this to do with Alex Faulkner?"
"I'm coming to that."
"You said – Faulkner owns casinos. Did he – persuade my father to play in them? To lose money?"
"I mean no such thing." Mr. Falstaff was flustered. "On the contrary, Faulkner seldom enters his casinos. But your father did get into debt for – well, rather a lot of money."
"I don't believe it. Why, the company – our house – "
"Everything appears to be intact, doesn't it? But Alex Faulkner owns your father's possessions just as surely as if he had signed the deeds."
"But why didn't I know? Why wasn't I told?" Charlotte was shattered.
"For the simple reason that I did not know myself until yesterday."
"But how can you be sure – "
"I'm satisfied that what Faulkner's solicitors say is true."
Charlotte got up from her seat, unable to sit still after such a revelation. "I – I can't believe it!"
"Nor could I. At first."
Charlotte's brain darted here and there, trying to absorb what this would mean to her. Then she swung round. "The insurance! Daddy's insurance!" She expelled her breath unsteadily. "Thank God for that!"
"I'm – afraid not."
"What do you mean?"
"Oh, Miss Mortimer, can't you see? This throws an entirely different light on your father's death. Once the police learn that your father was mortgaged up to the hilt, I doubt very much whether they'll be content with the Coroner's findings."
"You mean – you mean – you think Daddy – Oh, no! He – he wouldn't."
"In the circumstances, I think he might."

"What – circumstances?" Charlotte stared at him.

"Sit down, Miss Mortimer. I haven't finished yet."

Charlotte looked as though she might refuse, but eventually she resumed her seat, staring at the solicitor with wary eyes.

"I have in my possession a letter from Faulkner," said Mr. Falstaff slowly. "In it, he sets out a certain contract he made with your father in return for lending him a *vast* sum of money."

"What kind of a contract? Let me see the letter."

"All in good time, Miss Mortimer. Briefly, it waives your father's debts in return for – something else."

"Oh, do stop hedging. What 'something else'?"

"You, Miss Mortimer. You!"

"Me!" Charlotte sank back in her chair aghast. "What do you mean – *me*?"

Mr. Falstaff looked most unhappy. "Miss Mortimer, during our little talk I've tried to explain that Mr. Faulkner is a rather – remote figure. He cares little for anyone, and in consequence there are few women in his life. Nevertheless, he does realise that some day he will have to retire, and when that time comes he will require an heir, someone to carry on the organization after he is dead – "

"You – you mean – " Charlotte gasped disbelievingly, trying to make light of something that was too ludicrous to be true. "Good lord, what does he think I am? A brood mare?"

"Please, Miss Mortimer. This is no laughing matter."

"You're damn right. It's not. It's stupid, ridiculous! I can't believe that anyone in this day and age could have seriously considered something so – so barbaric! Me? Marry a man I don't even know? A man old enough to be my father!" She hesitated. "I'm presuming marriage is what he has in mind."

"Oh, yes. The solicitors were most definite about that."

Charlotte shook her head. "I suppose I should be flattered. He might have decided just to *use* me!"

"Miss Mortimer!"

"Well, it's madness!"

"Mr. Faulkner is a very determined man."

"Well, it's not on, and that's that."

"I'm afraid that's not that, as you put it."

"Why not?"

"I don't think you've really considered what this could mean, Miss Mortimer. Alex Faulkner owns you just as surely as he owned your father. Your house, your clothes, your car . . . Even the company."

"There's still the insurance."

"I doubt they'll pay out."

"But why should they suspect? You said yourself, you didn't know until Faulkner – "

"Miss Mortimer, I have my position to consider. They will have to be told. But even if I remained silent, Alex Faulkner would not."

"You mean – he would inform the police?"

"If you fail to agree to his plans, he might go to any lengths."

"The – the *swine*!" Charlotte felt almost physically sick. "Why is he doing this?"

"Because he wants you – as his wife."

"But why? Why me?"

"Perhaps your father – " He broke off. "I don't know. He's not looking for a woman he can love, Miss Mortimer. Just a mother for his son."

"My God, it's feudal!" Charlotte squared her shoulders. "Well, let him do his worst. Let him take the company – and the house – and the car! I can earn a living. I have a job already. I don't need his money, even if Daddy did."

She was refusing to consider the other implications behind all this. They were too painful to contemplate here, in this dry dusty office, in company with this dry dusty man.

Mr. Falstaff leant towards her. "Charlotte," he said, using her given name for the first time. "Charlotte, don't think too badly of your father. If you want my opinion, I think he did take his own life – "

"Because he couldn't face what he had done!"

"No. No, to try snd salvage what he had done. Charlotte, remember the insurance. He only took it out a few weeks before he died. Obviously, he thought if Faulkner got his money . . ."

Charlotte held her breath. "Do you think – "

"No. It's no use." Mr. Falstaff was very definite about that. "After receiving the – er – communication, I contacted Faulkner's solicitors by telephone. They stated emphatically that Mr. Faulkner is no longer interested in a settlement of the debt."

"But – but is that legal?"

"Well, it's not illegal. Not in the circumstances. It does involve a certain amount of moral blackmail, but that's not illegal either. Clearly, your father underestimated the man."

"What do you mean? What kind of moral blackmail?"

"Consider, Charlotte, what the press could make of your father's suicide. Are you prepared to have his name dragged through the mud?"

Charlotte shook her head. "If what you say is true, my father died because of me. Do you think he'd care about his name being smeared because of it? If it stopped Alex Faulkner getting what he wanted?"

Mr. Falstaff sighed wearily. "You forget – the contract."

"I signed no contract."

"No. But your father did."

Charlotte frowned. "Surely Faulkner would never publicise that! Good lord, it would involve him just as much as Daddy."

"Not necessarily. Charlotte, you don't realise, a man in Alex Faulkner's position can do almost anything without suffering the consequences. I've no doubt he owns more than one prominent editor of a national newspaper. Can you imagine how this could be portrayed? *The Price of Virginity*!

Business man settles Gambling Debts with his Daughter! The Infamous Games People Play!"

Charlotte caught her breath. "You're wasted here, do you know that?" she burst out on a sob. "You should be writing the headlines yourself!"

"I regret those were not my quotations," replied Mr. Falstaff quietly. "They were quoted to me."

Charlotte got up again and walked restlessly round the room. "He can't do this to me! *He can't!*"

Mr. Falstaff shrugged his thin shoulders. "I wouldn't bank on it, Miss Mortimer. Not unless you're prepared to shoulder the interest which might accrue."

Charlotte walked to the window and looked down on the busy London street. Her mind was in a turmoil. She could not take in all she had heard, and what she had taken in, she could not believe. She had heard of people owning other people, of course, who hadn't? But that her father should be among that assembly didn't bear thinking about. Who was this man who thought he held the power of life or death over people? What manner of man could he be to drive another man to sacrifice his own daughter for a game of cards? It was like some Victorian melodrama, only she was no Victorian. And he was a cold, heartless shell of a man, incapable of acquiring a wife for himself.

Swinging round, she said: "So where is he? This Alex Faulkner? I want to see him."

"He does not live in England," said Mr. Falstaff flatly. "And that will have to be arranged."

Charlotte's lips trembled. "Oh, yes, arrange it. I want to tell him to his face exactly what I think of him!"

Mr. Falstaff rose to his feet. "Oh, Charlotte, please! Don't act rashly. You're little more than a schoolgirl. Faulkner could eat you alive!"

"Oh, really? Not when I get through telling him what an inhuman beast of a man he is! What a pathetic imitation of a man he must be to get his kicks through manipulating others!"

Mr. Falstaff could see the unshed tears glistening behind her eyes, and he shook his head compassionately. "My dear child, stop tormenting yourself like this."

"What am I supposed to do? Accept it?"

"I think you may have to. There are worse fates."

"Are there?"

"Oh, yes. Once you have – er – provided the necessary heir to the Faulkner fortune, you will be free to leave. To get a divorce and live comfortably – *luxuriously* – for the rest of your life. Why, by the time you're twenty-one, you could be your own woman again."

Charlotte's dark brows grew together. "Did he say so?"

"It's in the contract."

"The contract!" Charlotte drew an unsteady breath. "Where is it? I think I have a right to see it."

Mr. Falstaff opened a drawer of his desk and withdrew a foolscap manilla envelope. He passed it across to her. "Take it home," he advised. "It's just a photo-copy, naturally. I'll telephone you tomorrow when I have some more information."

Charlotte fingered the envelope. "Just out of curiosity, where does Faulkner live?"

"He has an island, off the Greek mainland – Lydros. He spends much of his free time there. I should also tell you that he has homes – houses – in many of the capital cities of the world. There is his penthouse apartment overlooking Hyde Park, for example, and the town house he owns on the East Side of New York – "

"I don't want to hear about his possessions," retorted Charlotte bitterly. Then: "You – you can tell whoever it is you communicate with that I refuse to consider this matter any further until I get to meet Alex Faulkner."

Mr. Falstaff made a helpless gesture. "My dear, you don't *tell* Faulkner anything. You suggest."

"Then suggest it. But make sure you get it right." She uttered a sound which was half between a laugh and a sob.

"My God, imagine having to insist on meeting the man you're expected to marry!"

At three o'clock in the morning, Charlotte went downstairs and made herself some tea. She had been lying awake for hours, her mind far too active to allow her to rest, her nerves too stretched with the sense of apprehension which filled her. She couldn't believe what was happening to her, and yet it *was* happening, and there seemed little she could do about it.

She had cared for her father deeply, but the things she had learned about him the previous afternoon had shaken her to the core. Briefly she recalled the little she had known of his enjoyment in gambling, the few occasions when he had surprised her with a present, some gift in celebration of a horse which had beaten its opponents past the post. Had she been too young to see a deeper meaning behind it all? And, like a drug, had it gradually gained a stronger hold upon him? Encouraged no doubt by men like Alex Faulkner!

But whatever had possessed him to put his name to such an infamous document as that contract she had read with such loathing? How could he, even for a moment, have considered such a solution? And then to take his own life like that ... For now she felt convinced that that was what he had done. Some people said that suicides were cowardly, afraid to face life. In her present frame of mind, she was inclined to agree with them. Whichever way you looked at it, it was a horrible mess – on the one hand cheating her, and on the other cheating the insurance companies. It was as though the man she had known and loved had never even existed and it was a devastating realization.

Even so, she could not bear to think of what her father's erstwhile colleagues would say if they ever discovered to what depths he had sunk. Something, some inner sense of pride, made her flinch from their hidden laughter, from the pitying sympathy which would be hers if ever this got out. So – if she went through with this, she would be doing it for herself, and not for her father, she thought bitterly. Was Alex Faulkner so astute? How cynical was his assessment of his fellow man?

One of the capsules, which the doctor had given her to help her to sleep immediately after her father's death, brought oblivion towards dawn, and she awoke feeling headachy, and with a nasty taste in her mouth, around noon. At first, she couldn't imagine why she should have slept so late, and then the remembrance of the previous day and night's events came back to her, and she rolled over to bury her face in the pillow. If only she could just bury Alex Faulkner, she thought violently, and then kicking off the covers, she got up.

When she came downstairs about a quarter of an hour later, slim and pale in mud-coloured levis and a green tee-shirt, her silky hair gathered back with a leather hair-slide, she found Laura Winters, their daily, busily slicing vegetables into a saucepan. Laura was a West Indian woman in her thirties, divorced now, with two young children of her own to support. She occupied a flat in a block just round the corner from Glebe Square, and had been working for the Mortimers for the past five years. She looked relieved when she saw Charlotte, although she noticed the dark rings around the girl's eyes with some concern.

"I was beginning to wonder if I should wake you, Charley," she said, shaking her head. "You been staying out late?"

Charlotte shook her head. "No. I didn't sleep well, Laura. You okay?"

"Yes, I'm fine. I've got young Jessie off school with a stomach ache, but she'll be all right. Been eating too many of them plums, that's all. That tree in the garden has been full this year. I must have made more than fifteen pounds of jam."

Charlotte bit her lip. Her father used to love Laura's home-made jam. Going to the steel sink, she ran herself a glass of water and sipped it slowly, watching Laura's deft hands as she dealt with the onions and carrots. Then she said: "Have there been – any calls for me?"

Laura frowned. "Sure, and I was forgetting." Charlotte tensed. "That lady you was working for called." Charlotte relaxed again. "She said to tell you she doesn't get half the young men coming into the shop she used to do."

Charlotte acknowledged this with a slight smile, and Laura went on: "What's up with you? You're looking awfully pale. Not still grieving over your pa, are you? It don't do no good. He's gone. Life goes on. Just pull yourself together, Charley."

Charlotte put down her glass. "I – I may be going away, Laura," she said slowly.

"Going away?" Laura looked astounded. "Where would you be going?"

"I – don't know. Greece, maybe."

"Greece. And who do you know in Greece?" Laura looked sceptical.

"I don't know where I'm going yet," retorted Charlotte sharply. Then: "I'm sorry, Laura, but I just may have to."

Laura frowned over her task. "There's more to this than you're telling me. Are you sure you're telling me the truth? About last night, I mean. You've not gone and got yourself mixed up with some man, have you?"

Charlotte stifled an hysterical giggle. If Laura only knew! Shaking her head, she walked to the kitchen door. "Don't do much lunch for me, Laura," she said, opening it. "I'm not really very hungry."

Leaving the older woman to her speculations, Charlotte walked across the hall and into the comfortable lounge which overlooked the garden at the back of the house. It was unusual to have a large garden in London, but it had been one of the things her mother had most loved about the house. She had been a keen gardener, most content tending her plants and weeding the flower beds. Some of Charlotte's clearest memories were of her mother teaching her small daughter the names of some of the plants and how to look after them. Then Charlotte had gone away to school and soon afterwards her mother had died. Her father had told her that her mother's heart had never been strong, and a severe attack of bronchitis had proved fatal.

Now Charlotte opened the french doors and stepped out on to the paved patio. They had a man who tended the garden these days, and it was pleasant to come out here on a hot day and sit in the shade of the fruit trees. Not that she would be able to do this much longer, she thought with sudden depression. Whatever happened, the house would have to be sold. Besides, it was getting quite chilly out here. September was bringing mists and cool breezes, and the smouldering scent of burning leaves drifted from the garden next door.

Charlotte had bent down to examine a particularly large beetle which had somehow wedged itself between two of the paving stones when the doorbell rang. Expecting it to be a tradesman, Charlotte made no move to answer it, but then she heard footsteps behind her, and glancing over her shoulder she found a rather agitated Laura stepping out of the french doors.

"It's a man," she told the girl in a low voice, and Charlotte got jerkily to her feet.

"A man?"

"Yes. I've never seen him before, but he insists you'll know who he is. I didn't know what to do, so I've left him waiting in the hall. He says his name's Faulk – Faulkner? Is that right?"

CHAPTER TWO

A WAVE of blind panic swept over Charlotte at these words. "Faulkner? Are you sure?"

"As sure as I can be." Laura looked at her curiously. "Why? Who is he? He came in a big black limousine. Seems like he's not short of money." She paused. "Don't you want to see him?"

Charlotte passed a dazed hand over her forehead. *Did she want to see him?* Yes. But not like this. Not so – precipitately. Was that why he had come? The element of surprise to add to his attack?

"I – yes, I want to see him, Laura." Charlotte glanced down frustratedly at her jeans and tee-shirt. If he was standing in the hall, she could not pass him to get changed. "Mmm – show him into Daddy's study – well, *the* study, anyway. I must get changed. I can't see anyone like this!"

"Why not?"

The deep male voice so unexpectedly behind them startled both women, and Laura's huge brown eyes widened in dismay. For Charlotte, it was a moment of complete imbalance, and she stared at the man confronting her with almost childish indignation. The words "*How dare you*!" formed and disintegrated without being spoken as her astonishment at his audacity gave way to a sense of shock. If this was Alex Faulkner, he bore no slight resemblance to the man whose image she had created.

Her imagination had conceived an obese, repugnant individual, his body bearing witness to the excesses in which he indulged. A man whose appearance repelled those women he would want to attract, and who had to resort to blackmail to get himself a wife. The reality came almost as a relief.

This man was tall, around six feet, she guessed, with a broad muscular frame. His skin was darker than was normal for an Englishman, and she wondered if there was some Greek blood there somewhere. Straight dark hair lay thickly against his scalp, and grew in sideburns down to his jawline. He was not handsome, but his hard features did have a certain attraction. He was immaculately dressed for the city in a dark blue pinstripe suit, the jacket unfastened to reveal the matching waistcoat beneath, the pants moulding the powerful muscles of his thighs.

In those first few seconds, Charlotte found disbelief uppermost in her thoughts. This could not be Alex Faulkner, could it? No man who looked like he did, who had such superb self-confidence, whose eyes seemed to penetrate to the very core of her being, could seriously consider buying himself a wife. *Could he?*

Gathering herself with difficulty, she realized he was waiting for her to speak. Laura, too, was watching her strangely, and Charlotte felt the hot colour running up her throat to her face. Oh, yes, she decided, with sudden insight. This *was* Alex Faulkner. This was exactly the sort of thing he would do to disconcert her.

"I – you are – *Mr*. Faulkner?" she enquired coolly.

"That's right." His eyes assessed her insolently. "And you must be Charlotte."

Charlotte! Charlotte's indignation hardened. For a few moments she had allowed his appearance to disconcert her, and now he thought he had the upper hand. Well, he was wrong! This was still the man who had forced her father to sign that contract, still the man who had driven her father to his death! Bitterness surged inside her.

"What are you doing here, Mr. Faulkner?" she demanded.

"An unnecessary question, don't you think? As you asked to see me," he returned smoothly. Then he looked at Laura. "You can go. I want to talk to Miss Mortimer alone."

"I'll dismiss Laura, as and when I choose," exclaimed

Charlotte angrily, putting a detaining hand on the older woman's arm.

He inclined his head. "If you wish to discuss our affairs in front of your housekeeper, that's all right with me. However, don't you think she might find it rather embarrassing?"

Charlotte pressed her lips frustratedly together. Then she gave a helpless little shake of her head. "All right, Laura," she said, her hand falling to her side. "Thank you."

Laura moved reluctantly towards the french doors, glancing back doubtfully, and following her Alex Faulkner said: "You can fetch us some coffee – Laura, isn't it? Then you can reassure yourself that I'm not a rapist – or worse."

Laura's mouth opened in a gasp, but she said nothing, and Charlotte indicated that she should do as she had been asked. Then they were alone, and her heart refused to slow its exhausting pace.

Alex Faulkner turned and looked at her, then he gestured towards the french doors. "Shall we go inside?" he suggested coolly. "I would not expect you to want our conversation to be overheard."

"Don't you mean you don't want it to be overheard?" she burst out hotly, and his mouth turned down at the corners.

"My dear Charlotte, if you want to discuss your father's addictions out here, that's perfectly all right by me."

Charlotte glanced round apprehensively. Although his voice was deep, it was very clear and succinct, and he had spoken in just a slightly raised tone deliberately.

"Oh, come inside," she exclaimed angrily, and brushed past him into the lounge.

He followed rather more slowly, looking about him with evident interest, and unable to prevent herself, she said: "Assessing your property? I believe you'll get quite a good price for it these days!"

Alex closed the french doors and leant back against them. "You've decided to sell, then?"

"*I've* decided? Don't you mean you have?"

"No." Alex shook his head. "This house is yours, as is the company. They're of no value to me."

Charlotte stared at him. "What do you mean?"

"Exactly what I say. What possible use would I have for another house in London? But I would suggest you sold the company. You could always invest the money. I believe Faulkner shares are quite viable."

"What do you mean? What are you talking about?" Charlotte could feel panic rising inside her again. "Everything's yours, you know it is!"

"No. Everything's yours. Only *you* are mine."

Charlotte's gulping laugh was hysterical. "You can't be serious!"

He straightened, his features hardening. "I trust we will not have to go through all that. I understand your solicitor made the position perfectly clear to you yesterday."

"Perfectly clear? *Perfectly clear?*" Charlotte gulped again. "I won't marry you! I – I don't know you! And – and besides, I wouldn't marry the man who – who drove my father to kill himself!"

"Ah!" He thrust his hands into the pockets of his jacket. "So you've found out."

"What do you mean? Found out?"

"That your father's death was no accident, of course."

Charlotte gasped, "You mean – you mean you can stand there and tell me coolly that my father committed suicide, knowing that you were directly responsible – "

"I was not directly responsible," he interrupted coldly. "Was your father a machine? An automaton, controlled by my manipulations? *No!* He was not. He was a free and thinking individual. Gambling was second nature to him – "

"No!"

" – and the stakes were never too high for him! Good God, this isn't the first time he's gambled his soul away!"

"What do you mean?"

"Never mind." He breathed deeply. "So – as I say, he chose to play. He knew the rules, as well as anybody else."

"Oh, that's very easy for you to say, isn't it?" Charlotte stormed, her breasts heaving. "Do all murderers excuse themselves so easily?"

Alex's eyes, which she had thought to be dark brown, were now almost black, and shaded by thick black lashes guarded his expression. "I am not a murderer," he stated quietly. "I did not choose the stakes."

"What do you mean?"

"I mean that like all addicts, your father needed one more game – one more chance to win. He had nothing left, so – he chose you!"

"I don't believe you."

"I don't expect you to. Nevertheless, as you get to know me better, you will learn that I do not tell lies. Nor do I make rash statements which I cannot sustain. You belong to me, Charlotte, whether you like it or not, and you will marry me."

"Why? Why me?" Charlotte's forehead and palms were damp, and she could feel the trickle of sweat at the back of her neck. "Am I so desirable? Or are you one of those men who prefer *young* girls?"

If she had thought to arouse his anger, she was disappointed. A faint sardonic smile crossed his lips, and belatedly she recalled what Mr. Falstaff had said about crossing swords with this man.

"I have no preference," he said then, surveying her in a way which deepened her unease. "So long as you were not too repulsive and were capable of bearing a child, I had no objections."

Charlotte gasped, "You mean – you would be prepared to make love to any woman, just to get a son?"

"Oh, no, not any woman. You seemed eminently suitable. But I would hardly call the act we are to perform making love!"

Charlotte stepped back from his cold cynicism. "But – there must be dozens of women who – who would jump at the chance . . ."

"You flatter me." But he did not sound gratified. "However, the women who might, as you say, jump at the chance, are not the kind of women I would choose to be the mother of my son."

"How do you know what kind of woman I am?"

He shrugged. "The very fact that you are chafing at your fate reveals a certain independence of character. I like that."

Charlotte sniffed resentfully. "So – if I'd thrown myself into your arms, you'd have changed your mind?"

"Such a hypothetical question requires no answer. We're wasting time. Are there any questions you wish to ask?"

"I – I – "

Charlotte was still staring at him desperately when Laura knocked at the open door. Alex glanced round, saw the woman standing there, and indicated that she should place the tray on a low table near the couch.

"Is there anything else, Charley?" Laura looked anxiously towards the girl, who hardly seemed aware of her presence. Charlotte heard the words as if from a distance, and swung about.

"I'm sorry, Laura. No, no. That's fine, thank you."

"What time would you like lunch?" Laura persisted, obviously reluctant to leave them, but Alex intervened.

"Miss Mortimer will not be in for lunch," he stated firmly.

Laura's eyes widened in dismay. "Not in? After I made this good food? Is that right, Charley?"

Charlotte shook her head, trying to shake away the dazed feeling of unreality which had enveloped her with increasing speed since Alex Faulkner's arrival. "I – what? I don't know, Laura. Am I lunching out?" She turned to stare at Alex.

"Yes. We'll eat at my apartment," he replied, ignoring Laura's exclamation of protest. "Oh – and by the way." He glanced at Charlotte and then transferred his attention to the daily. "Miss Mortimer is getting married in a few days. She may wish you to stay on here, if she decides not to sell this house. Otherwise, she'll let you know."

"What? What's this?" Laura stared disbelievingly at the girl she had known for five years. "Is this true, Charley? You getting married? Why didn't you tell me?"

Charlotte swallowed convulsively. "It's not as simple as that, Laura." She cast a furious glance in Alex's direction. "Nothing's settled yet. Nothing's arranged."

"On the contrary, everything's arranged," returned Alex smoothly. "Your – er – your employer is a little – bemused by her good fortune, that's all."

"Why, you – " Charlotte bit back an epithet as realization of what a denial would mean struck her. This was really happening, he really expected her to go through with it. The moment of decision had come.

Laura waited for Charlotte to go on, but when she didn't, she said imploringly: "Charley, I don't understand all this. You never said a word to me." She looked Alex up and down. "I never seen this man before, and I don't think you did, too."

Charlotte felt as if she was nearing the end of her tether, and it was almost a relief to hear Alex say: "We've been – corresponding with one another. You know – pen-friends, that sort of thing. Miss Mortimer's father knew all about it. He – he would approve."

Charlotte clenched her fists and turned away, unable to meet Laura's accusing stare. Patently, she didn't believe Alex, but equally she had no proof to the contrary. Besides, sooner or later she would have to believe it. It would be an indisputable fact.

She heard Alex dismissing the West Indian woman, and then he gestured to the coffee. "I like mine black, with sugar, two spoons," he directed her coolly. "You might as well begin to learn your wifely duties here and now."

Charlotte sank down wearily on to the couch. "You really expect me to go through with it, don't you?"

"I *know* you will," he said, seating himself in the armchair opposite, legs apart, hands hanging loosely between. He had nice hands, she noticed inconsequently, long-fingered brown hands, rings on each of his little fingers. One was a kind of signet ring, gold, inset with a ruby; the other was filigree silver, thick and broad, a useful weapon in a fist fight.

"So," he said, deliberately intercepting her gaze. "Let us have the coffee, then perhaps over lunch you'll think of things you need to know."

Charlotte drank her coffee without tasting it. When she got to her feet, he rose also, and she looked at him apprehensively. "I – I need to change," she told him shortly.

"Very well. I'll wait here." He lounged into his chair again, but his eyes were watchful. "Don't be long."

Charlotte made no reply, her lips clenched mutinously as she left the room, slamming the door behind her. In the hall, she breathed deeply. She desperately wanted to escape, to run away from the situation that was developing without her volition. What would he do if she disappeared? Employ detectives to find her, without doubt. Where in the world would she be safe from a man like him? There was no answer to that.

Laura put her head round the kitchen door. She had obviously heard the slamming of the door and when she saw Charlotte she left the kitchen and came purposefully towards her. "What is all this?" she hissed impatiently. "What is that man doing here? I don't believe he knew your father."

"Oh, he did, believe me," Charlotte assured her wearily, realizing that she could not confide even in Laura. If she had to go through with this, no one must know at what cost. She could not bear sympathy on top of everything else. Somehow, she would do it, though *he* should not find it the easy path he imagined. And afterwards she would take him for every penny she could squeeze out of him!

"And you're thinking of marrying him?" exclaimed Laura, in dismay.

"Yes." Charlotte's tone was flat, but Laura didn't notice.

"And what about me?" she demanded. "You selling this house?"

Charlotte shook her head. "No. No. I don't know. I don't think so." She sighed. "Laura, you don't have to worry, whatever happens. I'll see you're all right. You and Jess and Billy. I – well, I just may keep this house on. I mean, you never know when a house can come in handy. You could be sort of – caretaker, if you like. I'd pay you, of course."

Laura folded her arms and shook her head. "There's more to this than meets the eye, Charley, and you know it. I wasn't picked off the banana tree yesterday. I ain't that green!"

Charlotte had to smile, even though she felt more like crying. "Laura, I've told you the truth. What more can I say?"

Laura sniffed. "All right, have it your way. I just never thought there'd come a time when my little Charley told me lies!"

"They're not lies, Laura." Charlotte spread her hands. "Honest to God, I'm not about to enter a harem or anything. He – " she gestured with her thumb, "he wants to marry me. Is that so strange? Am I so unattractive?"

"You're deliberately misunderstanding me, Charley. You know you're the prettiest girl I know. Too thin, of course, but that's natural, in the circumstances." Laura stared at the girl anxiously. "You going to be happy, Charley? This man got lots of money? He treat you good?"

"I – hope so," said Charlotte, bending her head so that Laura should not see the tears in her eyes. "Now – excuse me. I must get changed."

Charlotte was aware of Laura's reproachful eyes following her up the stairs, but there was nothing she could say to assuage her anxiety. Besides, she could not shoulder Laura's worries. She had more than enough of her own.

The car that waited outside for Alex Faulkner was a

chauffeur-driver Mercedes, the kind of car which hitherto Charlotte had only glimpsed around the town. A second man was seated beside the chauffeur, and both men got out at their approach.

"Vittorio Santos, my chauffeur," Alex indicated offhandedly. "And his brother, Dimitrios, my – bodyguard."

A bodyguard! As the luxurious vehicle rolled away, Charlotte stole a glance at the man seated so indolently beside her on the wide back seat which left fully two feet between them. Until then, she had not given a thought to the possibility that this man could well be a target for unscrupulous revolutionaries requiring a hostage. If – *when* – she became his wife, would she require a bodyguard as well?

His wife! Even those words were startling. Mrs. Faulkner! It didn't sound real. Not to her. And then other, more intimate thoughts entered her head. To be this man's wife would be to submit herself to his every demand. He would have the right to share her bed, to make love to her whenever he chose, to deny her even the smallest privacy.

She trembled violently. The intimacies between a man and a woman were as yet unknown to her. Oh, she had listened to the girls in the school dormitory at night whispering about their experiences. She had attended biology classes and had the whole sexual act explained to her in detail. But what was the spoken or written word when compared to actual experience? The whole thing seemed vastly overrated, and although she had had boy-friends and indulged in kissing and a little mild petting, she had never felt any urge to explore further. The very idea seemed slightly indecent to her. To imagine this man, this *stranger*, seeing her without her clothes. ... She shrank a little further into her corner. If it did come to *that,* and she supposed that one day it would have to, she would make sure she was adequately clothed in pyjamas or a nightdress, and safely under the bedcovers.

Alex's apartment temporarily allayed her fears in a surge of pure admiration. The rooms at the house in Glebe Square had not been small but these rooms were enormous – wide and spacious, with expanses of soft carpet where one could stretch at will. The lounge had long windows, with slatted blinds, there were soft velvet couches in shades of blue and green, modern Swedish-style furniture cheek-by-jowl with what were obviously antiques and silky off-white carpeting.

An elderly man greeted them. Alex introduced him as Potter and it soon became apparent that Potter was a resident at the apartment, catering for his employer should it be necessary, although there was an excellent service restaurant on the ground floor of the block, and caretaking in his absence. Alex introduced her to the old man as his fiancée, much to Charlotte's dismay, and it was Potter who suggested that she might like to see all the apartment.

To her relief, Alex said he had some telephone calls to make and disappeared into a room which Potter explained was his study. Then they went on a tour of inspection.

Charlotte had never seen such luxury. There were three bedrooms, all with colour televisions and hi-fi equipment as well as the usual fitted units. There was a panelled dining room with a long table capable of seating more than a dozen people in the soft, velvet-seated chairs. The kitchen, too, contained eating facilities, and was sleek and modern.

Charlotte asked, half reluctantly, which room Alex used, but Potter seemed to find nothing strange in this. Indeed, he had taken her arrival in his stride, and she wondered whether he found anything odd in his employer producing as his fiancée a girl he had never seen before.

"This is Mr. Faulkner's room," he said, indicating the second largest bedroom, a room designed in shades of coffee and cream, with thick apricot satin curtains at the window. All the rooms had bathrooms adjoining, and Charlotte looked into Alex's bathroom with a certain desperation. What had she expected to find here? she wondered, looking at the coffee-coloured bath and basin, the cream tiled shower cubicle. No man could imprint his personality on somewhere he used so fleetingly. The whole apartment was beautiful, but that was all it was. A shell – which only occasionally housed its occupant.

She entered the lounge again alone, Potter having excused himself to go to the kitchen, and found Alex lounging comfortably on one of the velvet couches examining some papers he had taken from a briefcase beside him. He looked up at her entrance, however, and thrusting the papers aside, got to his feet.

"I have ordered lunch to be sent up," he told her smoothly. "I hope you like roast beef and Yorkshire pudding. I always eat English food when I'm in England. It never tastes the same elsewhere."

"I don't think I could eat a thing," Charlotte retorted tautly.

"Nonsense." He shrugged his broad shoulders. "Food can be a delight as well as a necessity, and the restaurant here can be recommended. Your clothes reveal that you've lost weight. Perhaps we should do something about them this afternoon."

"What's wrong with what I'm wearing?" she demanded resentfully, looking down at the navy wool suit which she had last worn at her father's funeral. "I'll have you know this suit was made to my design at a boutique where I – where I worked before..."

"You haven't worked since your father's death," Alex stated calmly, revealing a closer knowledge of her affairs than she had imagined. "And many of the clothes sold there are cheap and badly finished."

Charlotte caught her breath. "You don't know that."

"I assure you, I do. Besides, you don't suit that flat shade of navy. Royal blue would suit you far better."

"Have – have you been spying on me?"

"Not personally, no. I left my binoculars in Greece."

"Don't make a fool of me!" Charlotte shifted restlessly. "Well? Have you had someone watching me?"

Alex sighed resignedly. "In my position it's necessary to

investigate everybody I come into contact with – "

"Oh, God! That's terrible!"

"But necessary, I do assure you."

Charlotte turned away, biting her lips. "I could never be like that."

"You may have to be," he replied quietly. Then, as the doorbell chimed: "This sounds like lunch."

They ate in the lounge from the folding table sent up from the restaurant, seated by the windows which allowed one a panoramic view far beyond the Thames, to the expanse of green which was Richmond Park. During the meal, Alex talked, general things mostly which Charlotte answered in monosyllables but which nevertheless relaxed her sufficiently to enjoy at least a part of the meal, and she guessed that this was his intention. A clear vegetable broth was followed by the roast beef he had promised, and to finish there was a chocolate sponge pudding. He smiled when Charlotte refused the dessert, and had a second helping.

"You must forgive me," he said, pouring custard from a jug. "Sponge puddings have always been my favourite form of dessert and I always indulge my weakness when I am in London. Henri, the chef downstairs, keeps this on his menu especially for me."

"I'm surprised you don't have a food taster," remarked Charlotte rather spitefully, and Alex's smile deepened.

"It may come to that," he conceded dryly. "Are you as venomous as you sound?"

Charlotte sighed frustratedly. "Well!" she said defensively. "Private investigators, bodyguards! It's archaic! I'm surprised they don't live in the apartment!"

"Oh, but they do," Alex told her mildly.

"But – we left them downstairs ..."

"I didn't want to alarm you," he replied, finishing the wine in his glass and getting up from the table wiping his mouth with the table napkin. "I thought we would take it slowly."

"Slowly! Slowly!" Charlotte stared at him angrily. "You call forcing someone to marry you taking it slowly?"

Alex shrugged, regarding the array of bottles revealed by the opening of the cocktail cabinet with apparent consideration. "I would suggest you started accepting that situation and considered the advantageous aspects of it."

"What advantageous aspects?"

Alex held up a bottle of cognac, but Charlotte shook her head quickly and with an indifferent gesture he poured some into a balloon glass. Then he walked back to where she was still sitting at the table in the window, cradling the glass in his hands.

"Let me tell you about Lydros, hmm?" He paused. "It is an island approximately fifty miles off the mainland of Greece, in the group of islands known as the Cyclades." He swallowed a mouthful of his cognac, ignoring Charlotte's apparent disinterest. "We are very lucky on Lydros – there is an adequate water supply and we are able to grow much of our own produce. Old Spiro Santos, the father of those two brothers who also work for me, makes wine, and it is rich and sweet, like the grapes from which it is squeezed."

"I'm really not interested," retorted Charlotte tightly, but Alex merely smiled that infuriating smile and Charlotte could have slapped him.

"You will be," he assured her. "You will be living there in a little less than two weeks. I have to leave for New York tomorrow. I shall be away approximately ten days. I hope to be back in England on the fourteenth and we are to be married on the fifteenth."

Charlotte's breath seemed to be stuck in her throat. "But why?" she appealed, his confidence panicking her all over again. "Isn't there anything I can say – anything I can do to make you change your mind?"

"No." His expression hardened abruptly. "You have the choice – marry me, bear my child, and, in possibly a year, I'll set you free. Deny me that right, and I will not be responsible for the consequences."

"You're – you're a beast! Inhuman!"

"Why? Because I choose to make you honour your father's agreement?"

"No. No, because – well, because you don't *need* to do this. You – " She bent her head. "You're an – attractive man. I'm sure you could find some other woman equally suitable – "

"Why should I go to the trouble of doing that when I already have you?" He put out a hand and lifted her chin, and she flinched from the touch of those hard impersonal fingers. "Do not alarm yourself, little one. I shall not trouble you often. Only as long as it takes."

"But – what if I don't – what if we can't – " Her voice trailed away as her cheeks blazed with colour.

His hand fell away. "It's all arranged. While I am in New York, you will have certain – tests. I have already had them."

"You mean – you mean to see whether – whether I can?"

"Yes."

Charlotte uttered a gasp of horror. "Well, I hope I can't!" She spat the words at him.

His sardonic smile returned. "Don't tempt me to find out for myself, Charlotte. As my wife, you will have certain rights. As my mistress, you would have none at all."

Charlotte could feel a wave of hopelessness sweeping over her. "But – but I know nothing about you," she protested bitterly.

"What do you want to know? I have not refused to answer your questions. I am almost forty years of age, almost senile, I suppose that seems to you," he added shortly. "My father was killed by terrorists when I was twenty-four, and my mother died soon afterwards."

Charlotte hid the shock the news of his father's death had given her. Until then, the simple precautions he took had seemed rather dramatic and ridiculous. But suddenly they were not, and she felt a reluctant sense of shame.

"I am of English-Greek extraction," he went on flatly.

"My grandmother on my father's side of the family comes from Eastern Macedonia. She is still alive and lives with me on Lydros."

Charlotte digested this uneasily. "Will she – continue to do so?"

"After our marriage, you mean? Oh, yes. Do not be alarmed. She does not live in my house. She has her own villa across the island."

Charlotte shivered, but she couldn't help it. The reality of it all was gradually getting through to her.

"Is – is it a big island?" she asked, in a low voice, not wanting to dwell on the thought of meeting his grandmother.

"Not big, no. About five miles long, and two miles across at its widest point." He finished his cognac, and as he lowered the glass he looked at her over the rim. "It is a beautiful island. I was brought up there. As a boy I learned to swim and fish from its beaches; I explored its caves, and got trapped by the tide, so that Spiro had to come with his boat and get me out. My father taught me how to sail. He bought me a dinghy, and I used to spend hours trying to get back into shore after the wind had changed." His smile was not sardonic now. "There are only a few people on the island, the Yannis, and the Philippis and the Santos. We are not troubled by tourists, and the rocky coastline makes it impossible for large vessels to get inshore. It is very hot – very white – very beautiful. The sea is an unbelievable colour, always warm and soft. At night the only sounds come from the cicadas. Then occasionally, just occasionally, they are silent, and the stillness is uncanny."

During those moments, as he looked at her, Charlotte felt the strength of his love for the island, and the faintest glimmer of anticipation stirred within her. She had never been to Greece, never been further than Brittany in the summer, and Switzerland in the winter. The picture he had painted of his home was very attractive, and she found herself wondering what it would be like to swim in a warm sea.

But then he moved, and all eager sense of anticipation fled. Her eyes dropped down over the hard muscular length of his body, and a terrifying numbness gripped her. To see and experience the delights of the island, she was expected to accept whatever this man chose to do with her. She had never slept with anyone before, much less a man, and to picture him sharing her bed was to picture indignities too great to be borne. And even then, if she could endure the humiliation of being used, she had nine months more, nine months when her body would swell out of all proportions with all the agonies of childbirth before she could make her escape....

CHAPTER THREE

THEY flew to Athens in the executive jet owned by the Faulkner corporation. Charlotte had never flown in a private plane before, and the difference between this high-priced luxury and the tourist accommodation she was used to was quite staggering. The main cabin resembled a comfortable lounge, with a thick carpet on the floor, and deep armchairs for relaxation. Adjoining the lounge was a bathroom, with bath and shower, while beyond this was a small bedroom where Alex told her he snatched a few hours' sleep on an overnight flight. The Santos brothers travelled with them, and another man whom Charlotte had met for the first time the day before. He was George Constandis, Alex's personal assistant, an older man, about sixty, Charlotte surmised, and it was obvious that Alex valued his opinion. What any of the men thought of her, she had no way of knowing. They were all extremely polite to her, but their faces revealed little.

Charlotte for her part spent the journey dreading its termination. The wide gold band which Alex had slid on to her finger that morning in the registrar's office at Caxton Hall weighed heavily on her hand, and her other fingers constantly sought the reality of its presence there, twisting it round and round. She felt different somehow, changed in some indescribable way, as though just by becoming his wife she had submerged her whole identity.

Of course, there were differences, physical differences. Alex did not like the coppery gold of her hair confined in any way, so now it fell in a heavy curtain about her shoulders. It was far too long, she thought, and she had intended to have it cut now that she had left school and acquired some independence. But Alex had been very explicit when it came to her appearance, and what he wanted of her.

Her clothes, too, had been chosen by him. Or at least, on his instructions she had presented herself at a certain salon in the West End where a woman who wore the most garish make-up Charlotte had ever seen produced a wardrobe for her which must have cost the earth. It seemed an unnecessary indulgence to acquire so many gowns which, if his plans came to fruition, within a few months would no longer fit her. But he was making the decisions, and she was feminine enough to enjoy possessing so many beautiful things.

Mrs. Laurence, the woman she had worked for at Bebe's Boutique, had been astounded to learn that Charlotte was getting married, and even more astounded when she learned who the bridegroom was. Very few people would actually recognize Alex Faulkner in the street, but almost everyone had heard of Faulkner International.

"Lucky girl!" had been Mrs. Laurence's comment, and for *lucky* Charlotte had read *clever*. Mrs. Laurence was a widow who had had a struggle to bring up her two daughters. She envied anyone to whom money was no longer going to be an anxiety. Charlotte had wished she could see things so simply.

Only Laura, of the people she had told, had expressed any doubts about her good fortune. But then Laura had been present at that first fateful meeting, and Charlotte could not convince her that she was doing the right thing. Charlotte had arranged that Laura should look after the house for her, but this had only increased Laura's suspicions. She could see no reason why Charlotte should want to retain such an expensive dwelling when she would be living thousands of miles away. In addition, as Alex had his own apartment in London, there would be no future need for the house in Glebe Square.

Charlotte had made some excuse about keeping it on for sentimental reasons, and Laura eventually had to accept it. But she had no way of knowing that Charlotte saw the house as a lifeline, a bolt-hole where, if things became too impossible,

stare at him with horrified eyes. "Charlotte," he said heavily, "don't be so – frightened of me."

"I'm not frightened of you," she lied chokingly.

"God – you are!" he muttered exasperatedly. "And lying about it isn't going to make it any easier for you."

"I don't know what you're talking about."

"Yes, you do." His fingers were hard through the fine material of her pants. "Charlotte, you're my wife now. That's an indisputable fact. And as I'm not going to allow you to get an annulment or anything, I suggest you start behaving like a normal human being. All this – this jumping around when I lay a hand on you, the fear in your eyes when you thought we might be staying the night in Athens, worrying about whether your nightgowns will arrive in time! My God, what am I? A monster or something?"

"What do you expect me to do? Welcome the knowledge that you're my husband? Be transported by delight at the thought of bearing your child? I hate you, Alex Faulkner, and I refuse to make things easy for you!"

"Easy for me? My God!" He released her and sank back in his seat. "All right, Charlotte, have it your own way. But on your head be it."

Charlotte felt a twinge of remorse. "I – what do you mean!"

"You want to keep everything on a business footing, that's okay by me."

Charlotte caught her breath. "I – I don't know I said that."

He turned his head sideways against the soft upholstery, looking at her. "You can't have it both ways, Charlotte. Either we can pretend, and make things easier. Or we can keep to the terms of the contract. Either way, it's all the same to me."

"What do you mean – pretend?"

His eyes narrowed. "Now what do you think I mean?"

Charlotte could feel the hot colour burning her cheeks. "Oh – oh, *no!*" she gasped. "How – how dare you suggest such a thing?"

He shrugged and looked away from her, staring straight ahead. "I was only thinking of you, believe me. But if that's not the way you want it. . . ." He paused. "At least behave civilly in public. That's one thing I insist upon, do you understand?"

Charlotte did not answer him.

She had never flown in a helicopter before, and in other circumstances she would have been delighted by the trip out over the blue green waters of the Aegean, south-east over dozens of small islands each shimmering beneath a haze of heat. To Charlotte's astonishment, Alex piloted the helicopter himself, and she sat between him and George Constandis, her thigh wedged against the hardness of his. It was hot in the helicopter, and Alex had loosened the top buttons of his shirt and pulled down his tie. He was sweating freely and the scent of his hot body came to her nostrils. She turned her head away, not wanting to be any more aware of him than she already was in this confined space, but she could not suppress the thought that later tonight his hard powerful body would take possession of hers.

The back of her own neck was wet, and the coppery hair clung in damp strands to her jacket. She longed for a shower and a change of clothes. The cream suit which had seemed so suitable in the coolness of London was far too thick for this climate. But until her suitcases arrived, she would have to content herself with what she was wearing. Even so, pushing more disturbing thoughts aside, she contemplated the contents of her wardrobe with increasing pleasure, realizing that the flimsy garments she had felt so unnecessary at the time of their purchase would no doubt find a use in conditions like these. She had not realized it would be so hot.

During the short flight, Alex and George Constandis spoke to one another through headphones. There were only two sets of these and although George had offered a set to Charlotte, she had refused, knowing that he would have more to say to her husband than she would herself.

About half an hour after take-off, the helicopter began to descend over an island situated on the rim of the group and shaped not unlike the letter C. Two curved headlands sheltered a bay which was almost landlocked, with only the narrowest of channels between the two. Charlotte could see now how impossible it was for any boat to land on the island, except perhaps a launch piloted by someone who knew the rocky channel and the currents present there.

The helicopter came in low over the bay and ahead of them Charlotte could see a sickle-shaped beach with sand that was bleached white by the sun. Tussocky grass surmounted shallow cliffs and then lying directly below them she saw the house. She guessed it was Alex's house. It was much bigger than the several cottages that clung about the headland at this side of the island, and its long low lines looked cool and inviting. There were trees close by, firs and cypress and olive trees, and beyond the immediate environs of the house came the sharp scent of a lemon grove.

The helicopter landed on wide lawns out back of the house, and the distinctive roar of its motor and the whine of its propellers brought several people out of doors to greet them. Three women in white aprons and a man dressed entirely in black stood shading their eyes against the glare of the sun, and Charlotte felt a tightening knot of nervousness inside her. Of course, these people looked after the house. Foolishly, she had not considered servants.

The propellers slowed, and Alex took off his earphones and unfastened his seat straps. Then he slid back his door and climbed out, extending a hand to assist Charlotte to alight. She accepted his help reluctantly, putting her hand into his with some misgivings, but the pressure he exerted was cool and indifferent.

To her relief it was slightly cooler here, the breeze off the water giving the air a deliciously salty tang. She looked away to her left where the gentle undulation of the land gave way to deeper water and couldn't suppress a surge of pleasure at her surroundings. She had never seen anywhere more delightful, and the island at least lived up to her every expectation.

Then Alex was walking forward towards the small group gathered on the terrace beneath cool white columns of stone, and his expressive backward glance sent Charlotte hurrying after him. Of the women, two were young and one was elderly, while the man was of middle years. They greeted Alex warmly, shaking his hands and chattering away in their own tongue. Nevertheless, their eyes, particularly those of the younger women, strayed often in Charlotte's direction and embarrassment swept over her again.

Then Alex drew her forward, his hand firm at her elbow. "Charlotte, I'd like you to meet our staff here at the Villa Lydros." To her surprise he turned to the man first, standing to attention before them. "This is Cristof, our – *chef de cuisine*." The man bowed and he turned to the three women, the oldest first. "And this is Maria – and Sophia and Tina." The younger women bobbed and Charlotte glanced helplessly at Alex, but he was not looking at her.

"Er – how do you do?" she managed awkwardly, and the two girls exchanged giggles.

Maria, probably the housekeeper, Charlotte thought, gave them a quelling glare. Then she extended her hand to Charlotte. "*Kalispera,* Kyria Faulkner," she welcomed her politely. "*Parakalo. Embros.*"

Charlotte glanced at Alex once more and this time he encountered her gaze. "Maria is asking you to enter the house," he told her quietly. "Go ahead. I must speak to Constandis before he leaves."

"He's leaving?" Charlotte's mouth was dry.

"This is supposed to be our honeymoon," remarked Alex dryly. Then he shook his head. "Go with Maria. You'll find she speaks quite reasonable English. They all do – I taught them myself."

With slightly nervous steps, Charlotte followed the old woman across the cool terrace and into the house through sliding glass doors. The coolness inside was almost chilling, and she realized that although the walls of the building were thick, this coolness was the result of a very efficient air-conditioning system.

A cool stone hall extended through to the front of the house, widening here to run the length of the terrace. Arched doorways opened off the hall giving tantalizing glimpses of white-walled rooms which relied for their colour on hand-woven tapestries and pottery in brilliant shades and designs. Couches and chairs were mostly of leather or sheep and goat-skin, and self-coloured rugs were strewn across the polished wood-blocked floors. Beyond the terrace at the front of the house, Charlotte could see the cliffs and the curve of the bay, and through the open doors she could hear the murmur of the sea as it curled along the rock-strewn headland. The beach she had seen from the air was hidden below the cliffs, but she guessed there would be a path down to it.

Shallow steps out of the hall brought them to a slightly higher level where a circular table and chairs with curved arms pronounced this to be the dining area. Although all the furnishings Charlotte had seen so far were plain and functional, they had a certain style and elegance, fitting accoutrements to this spacious split-level bungalow that far surpassed anything she had imagined.

The old servant Maria said little, merely indicating a particular tapestry here or a pottery urn spilling over with exotic blossoms there; small evidence of her own pride in her surroundings.

Beyond the dining area, another hall extended into the west wing of the house. Here several doors were closed against them, but Maria led the way confidently to the last of these, and turning the handle ushered Charlotte into what she guessed correctly to be the master bedroom.

It was an enormous room, but dominated by an equally enormous four-poster bed which occupied a central area. Easily six feet across, and longer than average, it was flanked by furniture of comparable size – a huge tallboy, a massive double wardrobe, and a dressing table with carved legs. Long windows stood wide to the scents from the garden at the side of the house, long wild silk curtains in a delicious shade of green moving slightly with the breeze. The floor was wooden as before, but the rugs here were white and soft, matching the silken covers on the bed.

"Is good, *kyria*?" suggested Maria shyly, and Charlotte could not deny her. It was the most beautiful room she had ever been expected to sleep in.

"Thank you, Maria, it's delightful," she said, dropping her bag and the vanity case on to a chair and moving across the room. A bowl of arum lilies occupied a position on the table beside the bed, and she touched their waxy petals with a certain sense of poignancy.

Maria bustled across the room and opened two more doors. "Bathroom, dressing room," she indicated smilingly, obviously pleased by Charlotte's appreciation. "When suitcases arrive, Sophia will unpack for you."

"I can unpack my clothes," Charlotte protested, peering into the dressing room which was easily as big as her bedroom had been at Glebe Square. It possessed a bed too, and she wondered why.

"Sophia will unpack for you," said Alex's voice, unexpectedly deep and male after Maria's gentle tones. "Can we have some coffee, Maria? I'm sure my wife is tired after the journey."

Charlotte moved awkwardly back into the bedroom as Maria smiled and went away, and Alex closed the door behind her with a definite little click.

"Well?" he said, surveying her unsmilingly. "So you like my house."

In this at least Charlotte did not have to dissemble, and she nodded, glad of the respite from other, more terrifying topics. "No one could do otherwise," she answered truthfully. "It's exactly the sort of place people dream of owning."

"Is it?"

Alex flexed his shoulder muscles rather wearily and then, to her dismay, sat down upon the side of the bed. He took off his jacket and tie, throwing them carelessly aside, and then stretched back on the silk coverlet, his arms above his head.

Then he became aware of how apprehensively Charlotte was watching him, and a certain cynicism invaded his expression. "Not yet, Charlotte," he told her, with infuriating perception. "Not when Maria might come back at any moment. I shouldn't like to shock her."

Charlotte glared at him frustratedly. "Oh, you – you – I'm going to take a bath!"

"There's no lock on the bathroom door," he remarked lazily, closing his eyes. "But don't worry, I won't come in."

"See you don't." Charlotte snatched up her vanity case and marched towards the bathroom door. Then she hesitated, some of her assurance dwindling away. "You – you really won't come in, will you?"

Alex's eyes opened impatiently. "No, I really won't come in. *This* time!"

It was marvellous to strip off her clothes and get into cool water. The glass shelves above the vast circular bath were filled with crystal flagons of bath essence and body lotions, boxes of talç and dusting powders, all manner of fragrances intended to make bathing a more delightful experience. Charlotte sprinkled the bath essence sparingly. She wanted no tempting perfume clinging to her skin, inviting Alex to sample that silent inducement. Nevertheless, she did linger in the scented water, hardly daring to look beyond the evening ahead.

She heard sounds from the bedroom, and presently there was a tap at the bathroom door. Her heart leapt into her throat, and she snatched up the sponge to hold against her breast. "What – what do you want?"

Alex's voice was cool and flat. "The coffee's arrived. I just thought I'd let you know."

"Oh! Oh, well, thank you." Charlotte cleared her throat. "I – I shan't be long."

"Be as long as you like," replied Alex, without interest. "I'm going to get something rather more stimulating."

Charlotte frowned. What did he mean? Where was he going? She opened her mouth to speak, but the sound of the bedrooom door slamming behind him warned her that she would be wasting her time.

By the time she emerged from the bath and had dried herself on one of the thick towels, and then dressed in the clothes she had just taken off, the coffee had cooled considerably. But it was still very refreshing. It was the Turkish variety, very strong and very black, and it was exactly what she needed after the enervating relaxation of the bath. Maria had also provided sweetmeats, tiny sticky confections, made of sugar and marzipan, to have with the coffee, but Charlotte couldn't face them.

By the time she had drunk two cups of coffee, and unpacked the contents of her vanity case, setting out her few cosmetics rather incongruously, she felt, on the dressing table, the light was beginning to fade. Walking to the long windows, she looked out on the shadowy garden, smelling the perfume from some night-scented blossom, and hearing the murmur of the sea from the cove. Dozens of insects were visible in the light that streamed from windows back along the villa, and when one particularly large moth with soft velvety wings flew close to her window, Charlotte stepped quickly backward and closed the panes.

Immediately the room felt airless, and she looked round anxiously. Near the door, a switch intimated the presence of electric lighting and she walked towards it with relief and turned it on. But no light ensued, only a curious humming sound, and after a moment's panic she realized she had turned on the air-conditioning. Breathing deeply, she noticed a lamp beside the bed. Surely she could not go wrong there.

The lamp cast pools of shadow in the lovely room. She

started as an army of insects began throwing themselves at the window panes, and feeling tension increasing inside her she went and quickly drew the curtains.

She glanced at her watch. It was almost eight o'clock and she had not eaten since early that morning. Alex had arranged for a champagne lunch to be served aboard the plane, but apart from a glass of the bubbly liquid, which she had not really enjoyed, she had had nothing. If Alex had noticed her lack of appetite, thank goodness he had not commented upon it in front of the other men, but now she was beginning to feel decidedly faint.

When a knock came at the door, she jumped once more, and instead of inviting whoever was outside to come in, she went and opened the door herself. One of the young women she had met earlier stood outside, either Sophia or Tina, she wasn't sure which.

"I have come for the tray, *kyria*," she said politely, her dark eyes appraising Charlotte anew. "And Kyrios Alexandros asks that you join him in the *saloni*."

"*Alexandros?*" Silently, Charlotte repeated the word. Then realizing she was still being observed rather closely, she said: "Thank you. Will you show me where the – er – *saloni* is?"

Inclining her head, the girl gestured along the hall. "If you go to the hall, *kyria*, you will find it easily."

Charlotte nodded, stepping back into the room as the girl excused herself to pass her and get the tray. She didn't seem half so friendly as Maria, and Charlotte was not easy in her presence. After the girl had gone, Charlotte examined her appearance critically. Apart from eyeshadow and lipstick, she was wearing no make-up, but in this heat too much make-up would soon cake upon her skin. Besides, she seldom wore a foundation base and usually only creamed her face night and morning.

Lamps were lit along the corridor which led back into the main hall. The table was laid in the dining area, and Charlotte couldn't help admiring the finely woven lace mats and shining silver and crystalware. She could smell food, and her stomach was protesting noisily as Alex appeared through the arched doorway to the right of the shallow stairway.

To her surprise she saw that he had shed the dark suit he had worn for their wedding and their subsequent journey, and was now coolly relaxed in cream silk pants and a dark blue silk shirt. The shirt was open at the throat to reveal a tiny gold medallion suspended on a fine gold chain, and she could see the brownness of his skin.

Apprehending her astonishment, he said: "You forget, this is my home."

Charlotte, still embarrassed by the uncontrollable impulses of her stomach, managed to shake her head. "I didn't realize you had changed, that's all."

Alex gestured to her to enter the lounge ahead of him, and as she passed him, he said quietly: "The room you are occupying was never *my* room. I usually sleep in much less elaborate surroundings."

Charlotte glanced at him over her shoulder, her heart hammering at the look in his eyes. But then he moved away from her to where a tray of drinks resided on a low carved table, and she was able to regain a little of her composure.

"What will you drink?" he enquired, raising dark eyebrows. "Gin, scotch, vodka? What do you prefer?"

Aware of the emptiness of her stomach and the fragility of her control over the blind panic which was threatening to engulf her, Charlotte refused to consider anything alcoholic. "Er – do you have a fruit juice?"

Alex regarded her with exasperation. "Surely you do drink something! Sherry perhaps, or Martini?"

"I do – occasionally take a drink," she conceded jerkily, "but right now I'd prefer a fruit juice, if you don't mind."

"But I do mind. I mind very much. And as you're my wife now, perhaps I should insist that you join me in having a gin and tonic." Then, noticing the tautness of her whole body, the stiff way she held herself, as if afraid to relax in his presence, he sighed. "All right. Orange or lemon?"

"Orange juice, please." Charlotte twisted her hands together. "Er – do you think my luggage will be long?"

Alex handed her a glass of freshly squeezed orange juice, clinking with cubes of ice. "Not long. Vittorio and Dimitrios should be here soon after dinner. I'm sorry you couldn't change, too, but there'll be plenty of time for you to wear the clothes Verna chose for you."

Charlotte took the glass he proffered and sipped at it nervously. It was very cold and faintly sharp. Alex indicated the couch beside her.

"Sit down," he directed, turning from the tray with his own glass in his hand, liberally filled, she saw with dismay.

Charlotte sank down weakly on to the couch. In truth her legs felt none too steady at that moment.

"Did you enjoy your bath?" he asked, taking up a position before an ornamental trellis where jasmine twined. His alien ancestry seemed peculiarly pronounced this evening in these lamplit surroundings, his darkness accentuated by the white walls of this particularly Greek apartment.

Charlotte concentrated on the liquid in her glass as she replied: "Very much, thank you. I – I used some of the bath essence. I presumed that would be in order."

"Use what you like. This is your home."

"My home!"

She echoed his words bitterly, but Alex chose to ignore it. "You are at liberty to go wherever you choose, to treat this place as you think fit. If you have been used to going out a lot – to night clubs and theatres, no doubt you'll find it dull. But I own quite a comprehensive library, and George had orders to obtain the latest best-sellers from both sides of the Atlantic so that should you enjoy reading, you would not be short of books." He paused, swallowing half the liquid in his glass. "Apart from that, during the day there is swimming and sailing, walking if you feel so inclined, and always the sun."

Listening to him, Charlotte thought his words spelled a

prescription for the kind of life she would have happily accepted with the man she loved. But always here, overlaying everything with its ominous presence, was the real reason for her being here, and no amount of reassurance could make her forget it.

To her relief, Maria appeared a few moments later to announce that dinner was served. They carried their drinks up to the dining table, and were seated opposite one another, across that gleaming expanse of polished oak.

It was Charlotte's first taste of Greek cooking and it smelled so appetising that she was able to ignore for a while at least the tortuous turnings of her mental processes. Stuffed tomatoes, and tiny sardines, proved sufficient hors d'oeuvres to lean meat kebabs, served on a bed of vine leaves filled with rice. It was rich food, and the meat was oilier than she was used to, but it tasted delicious. Fresh fruit and cheeses were served as a dessert, and Charlotte decided to choose a peach to sweeten her mouth. She had had a glass of glowing red wine with the meal, noticing overtly that Alex had drunk several glasses himself, but she refused the liqueur he suggested with their coffee. The approach of night caused Charlotte to spill some of her coffee into the saucer, and she was aware of Alex watching her with undisguised impatience.

The launch arrived as they were drinking their coffee, and Alex excused himself to go and speak to the men. Presently the other young woman she had been introduced to earlier appeared with her suitcases, but when Charlotte got half out of her seat to take them, she shook her head.

"I have the keys, *kyria,*" she said rather more amicably than her contemporary had spoken before dinner. "I will attend to it," and Charlotte had subsided again rather resignedly.

She was left alone for fully half an hour, and by the time Alex reappeared, she had left the table and returned to the room they had occupied earlier. She couldn't sit down, however, and wandered about restlessly, her mind filled with a sense of dread.

It was a beautiful room, as were all the rooms she had seen so far, with its soft goatskin couches covered with attractively embroidered cushions. A wall cabinet revealed a collection of wood carvings which seemed strangely alien to this environment, but which nevertheless blended into the scheme of things. The jasmine-covered trellis cunningly concealed loudspeakers from another hi-fi system, and remembering their ubiquitous presence at the London apartment, she couldn't help but wonder what kind of music Alex enjoyed.

When he at last came back he found her standing hesitantly beside the tray of bottles, pondering the advisability of taking something for her nerves. His suede-booted feet had made little sound, but still she swung round, sensing his presence.

"I apologise for taking so long," he said, leaning against the framework of the doorway, watching her. "Sophia has unpacked your suitcases now, though, and you can go to bed when you like." His lips tightened as he took in her wary alertness. "What are you doing? Thinking of getting drunk to face the ordeal?"

His voice was harsh, and Charlotte quickly put some space between her and the alcohol. "I – no," she denied abruptly. Then, rather ludicrously, she realized: "I've noticed you like music. Who are your favourite composers?"

Alex stared at her as if she had suddenly taken leave of her senses. Then he straightened away from the wall, shaking his head. "Would you believe – Brahms and Liszt?" he demanded savagely. "Oh – go to bed, Charlotte. Get out of my sight! Before I decide to really give you something to stare at me like that about!"

Charlotte sustained his cold gaze for perhaps thirty seconds, fighting the desire to run from this place. But finally it was too much for her, and with a muffled sob, she brushed past him and out of the door, walking jerkily up the steps from the hall and down the corridor to her room.

Once she was there, the painful humiliating tears would not be denied, and she sank down on to the bed and sobbed until her whole body felt drained and aching. Then she dragged herself up again and stared about her. Her suitcases had disappeared, but inside the huge wardrobe the row of her clothes almost filled the empty space. A nightgown had been tentatively laid across the bed where the silken coverlet had been folded back to reveal real satin sheets.

Her breathing ragged, Charlotte slowly undressed, alert to every sound outside the door. But no one came as she washed and cleaned her teeth, and then put on the flimsy garment. Fortunately it was not transparent, but its clinging folds left little to the imagination. She ran a swift brush through her hair, and careless of which side she slept, climbed between the sheets of the huge bed.

She hesitated a long while over turning out the light, but eventually decided that she did not want to see him come into her room. If she closed her eyes very tightly, he might even believe that she was asleep and allow her twenty-four hours' grace. She thought it was strange that his pyjamas had not been laid out on the bed, too. After all, everyone expected him to sleep with her.

Then she closed her eyes, too tired to think any more, too weary of her own cowardice and his brutality to care what happened to her. And when she opened her eyes again, sunlight was streaming brightly through the green silk curtains.

CHAPTER FOUR

CHARLOTTE had bathed, and was dressing in white cotton pants and a sleeveless yellow shirt, when Tina brought her breakfast on a tray. The Greek girl greeted her politely as she had the night before, but her probing eyes sought the scarcely-tumbled covers of the bed. Charlotte guessed that within a very short time everyone at the villa would know that the master of the house had not spent the night in his wife's bed.

She took the tray and dismissed the girl rather abruptly, irritated by her knowing stare. After she had gone, Charlotte carried the tray to the bedside table, and sitting down examined its contents. The meal provided was a mixture of English and continental dishes, there being cereal, and bacon and eggs, as well as warm croissants with honey. She chose to sample the croissants, her still-uneasy stomach rejecting the grilled food, but she was hungry and she enjoyed what she had.

Since awakening, she had firmly refused to consider why Alex had chosen to stay away from her the night before, but now, with breakfast over and the day stretching emptily ahead of her, her curiosity could no longer be denied. Getting up from her bed, she walked across to the windows and thrusting them open gazed out with troubled eyes.

It was a beautiful morning, the air still deliciously fresh and cool. Even so, the distant headland was already shrouded in mist heralding another hot day. The sky was the palest of blues, shading to turquoise as sea and sky melted into one another. The water in the bay looked green and inviting, and even as she watched a small craft with white sails drifted out from the shelter of the cliffs. It was a narrow-hulled racing vessel, the kind of single-handed craft her father had been sailing the day he met his death. A lump came into her throat. She must never forget that tragedy, or her husband's part in it.

She straightened away from the windows. That was her husband out there, she was sure of it, and if it was there was no reason why she should not do a little exploring on her own. She hesitated a few moments over the tray, but then decided to leave it where it was. She did not wish to alert Maria and the others to her movements.

Leaving her bedroom, she walked along to the wide main hall. The double doors at the front of the building stood open this morning, and beyond the terrace, a path led towards the cliffs. Feeling rather like a convict who is suddenly presented with a means of escape and doesn't quite know what to do with it, she left the villa, and walked across the grassy cliff top to its edge. Looking down, she realized it would be possible to climb down to the cove, but not wanting to indulge in such childish antics, she looked round for the path. Sure enough, it sloped away to her right, winding in and out of the outcrops of rock that provided a natural protection against sliding feet.

The sails of the yacht were some distance out in the bay now, nearing the break in the headland, and she wondered with a reluctant sense of anxiety whether Alex intended negotiating the channel. Then she determinedly thrust her misgivings aside. What did it matter to her what he did? Or whether he was endangering his life? He meant nothing to her, no more than she did to him.

The wedge heels of her sandals sliding a little on the dusty surface of the path, Charlotte slowly began the descent into the cove, keeping a wary eye on the yacht. If Alex should decide to turn back, she should have plenty of time to reach the house before he landed.

Once on the fine sandy beach, she looked about her with interest. The rocky backcloth of the cliff was honeycombed with caves, some of which disappeared under the water at the point where the beach dwindled into a rocky promontory. A boathouse, set on stilts, was built at the far end of the beach, and a wooden jetty ran out from it into deeper water. From the beach, it was also possible to see another cove further round the headland, where a cluster of cottages, gleaming whitely in the sun, signified a small village. A few boats were drawn up between the rocks, and some children were playing in the water. But there was no means of access from here. To reach the village on foot, one would have to climb the cliff again and cross a stretch of headland.

Kicking off her sandals, Charlotte walked to the water's edge and allowed the tiny waves to curl about her toes. The water was like silk, soft and warm, and grains of sand tickled her feet. She bent to roll back the cuffs of her trousers and almost jumped out of her skin when Alex said: "Good morning, Charlotte!" from somewhere behind her.

She swung round, startled, jerking upright to find him standing only a few yards away from her on the beach. His only garment was a pair of fraying denim shorts that left the hairy expanse of his chest and long powerful legs bare. She had not seen him without the civilizing influence of shirt and trousers before, and as the shorts only reached somewhere slightly below his navel, there was little of him she could not see. He looked big and intensely masculine, the night's growth of beard still darkening his jawline, and Charlotte felt a peculiar tightening in her stomach.

Then her eyes darted revealingly to the yacht, still out in the bay, and following her gaze, he said: "I'm sorry to disappoint you, but that's Dimitrios. He enjoys sailing, too."

Charlotte looked round for her sandals, more for something to do than actually needing them. "There was no need to come creeping up on me," she retorted. "I – I was just taking a walk, that's all."

Alex hooked his thumbs into the low waistband of his shorts. "And I was just cleaning the launch's carburettor!" he returned, and when she still looked sceptical extended a hand for her to see the oil on his fingers. Charlotte felt somewhat chastened, and he went on: "Did you sleep well?"

Her cheeks burned. "I – yes. Very well, thank you."

"Good. You look less – strained this morning."

Charlotte brushed sand off her toes. "You – that is – you didn't – "

" – come to bed?" he finished for her. "No. Not to your bed, at least."

Charlotte's eyes were troubled as she glanced up at him. "I – why not?" Perhaps he had changed his mind after all. Her heart lifted.

But Alex was looking cynically at her. "Why do you think?" he asked mockingly. Then, more soberly: "I've told you, Charlotte, I'm not a monster. I realize this has been a tremendous upheaval for you, that you need time to get used to the situation – to *me!*"

Charlotte licked her lips. "How – much time?"

"As long as it takes," he returned flatly. "Now, will you stop behaving as if I'm about to leap on you, strip off your clothes, and take you, here – on the sand."

Charlotte quivered. "If – if this is supposed to be some kind of an apology – "

"*Apology*?" he echoed impatiently. "Like hell, it's an apology! It's a stay of execution, that's all!" And with that he turned and stalked away towards the boathouse.

Charlotte felt no further desire to remain on the beach, and she scrambled up the cliff path, arriving hot and dishevelled at the villa. She encountered Maria in the hall, and the old housekeeper looked with dismay at her dust-smudged pants and flushed cheeks.

"Is something wrong?" she exclaimed, but Charlotte shook her head.

"No, nothing. I went down to the beach, that's all."

"Ah." Maria folded her hands together. "You were looking for Kyrios Alexandros."

"No, I was not," Charlotte contradicted her sharply. "And

now, if you'll excuse me, I need a wash . . ."

Charlotte spent the rest of the morning in her room, refusing to admit what a futile exercise that was. After all, Alex was not in the villa. She could quite easily have sunbathed on the patio, or walked in the gardens among cool olive trees, but instead she chose to hold herself apart from the rest of the household.

The bed had been made in her absence, and kicking off her sandals, she stretched her length upon it, staring up mutinously at the softly moulded ceiling above her head. Her thoughts were confused after the things Alex had said to her. While there was a certain relief in his so-called stay of execution, there was also a bitter sense of insecurity. How long was she expected to live in this state of almost suspended animation, constantly aware of that impending approach of disaster?

In spite of the turmoil of her thoughts, towards midday she must have slept, because she awakened with a start, sure that someone else was in the room with her. She blinked her eyes, looking towards the door, but could see no one. Then the shadow by the window attracted her gaze and she saw Alex standing there, looking broodingly towards the horizon. His back was partially turned to her, but in denim trousers and a cotton sweat shirt he was less aggressively masculine.

Charlotte levered herself up on her elbows, resenting the way he had walked uninvited into her room, had watched her as she was sleeping. Had she really no privacy here?

"What do you want?" she demanded, and he turned slowly to look at her.

"So – you're awake." His appraisal was without feeling. "It's lunchtime. I came to tell you."

Charlotte sat upright, crossing her legs lotus fashion. "Sophia could have told me," she said shortly. "Or is this little exercise intended to show me that you're not waiving *all* your rights as a husband?"

Alex's lips tightened. "Don't fence words with me, Charlotte. You haven't enough weapons." He paused, moving away from the window. "And in future, I do not expect to find you sulking in this room all day."

"What am I supposed to do? Twiddle my thumbs on the patio?"

"You know perfectly well that there are advantages to living here," he told her quietly.

"What advantages? I must have missed them!"

Charlotte refused to be quelled even though her heart was hammering at her temerity. But Alex was no feeble adversary.

"Charlotte, you do realize what you are inviting, don't you?" he suggested dryly, and all desire for provocation left her.

Swinging her legs to the floor, she got off the bed, smoothing the creases out of her pants. "If – if you'll leave the room, I'll not be long," she said, holding up her head, and to her relief he moved towards the door.

"Very well, if you insist." He opened the door. "Wear something green. It suits you."

Charlotte's jaws clamped together as he closed the door. His meaning had been unmistakable, and she was greatly tempted to throw something at him. But he had gone, and for that she should be thankful.

By the time Charlotte appeared at the dining table, she had showered and changed into a full-skirted dress of pale blue silk which swirled about her slender legs as she walked. The style was more adult than anything she had worn before, and ignoring Alex's instructions she had piled her hair up on top of her head.

Alex was already seated at the dining table, studying the contents of the glass he was holding, but he rose at her approach and politely held the chair until she had sat down. When they were both seated he picked up the small bell beside him and rang it.

Tina served them with fresh melon, and when they were alone again, he said: "This afternoon, I'll show you the island.

Then you'll have no excuse for feeling bored."

Charlotte pressed her lips together, staring down rather uncomfortably at her plate. It wasn't true that she had been bored. Indeed, it had been a great temptation to remain out in the sunshine, but indignation and resentment had driven her indoors. She had no reason to tell him this, of course, even if her conscience did trouble her somewhat. Though why it should when his did not appear to trouble him, she could not comprehend.

"You do swim, I suppose?" he questioned, when she made no comment, and Charlotte nodded her head. "Good. Bring a swimsuit. There's a cove I know where the water is more than twenty feet deep."

Charlotte swallowed a mouthful of melon, and then said: "You don't have to entertain me, you know. I – I'm quite capable of entertaining myself."

Alex regarded her resignedly. "Charlotte, I *know* I don't *have* to entertain you. But as I have some free time and you are a stranger here ..." He pushed his half empty plate aside, and she glimpsed the impatience in his eyes. "For God's sake, girl, can't you even stand the sight of me?"

"Would you expect me to do so?" Charlotte defended herself. "I didn't create this situation, you did! Why should I –"

"Your father created this situation," Alex retorted coldly. "Never forget that!"

"Do you think I could?"

Charlotte would have left him then, she was on the point of thrusting back her chair and rushing back to the bedroom, when his hand descended on her wrist, holding her in her seat with sheer strength.

"Don't go," he said, and his tone was quietly commanding. "All right. If you'd rather not spend the rest of the afternoon with me ..." He shrugged. "I won't force you."

Charlotte stared at him with a mixture of pain and compassion. She was reprieved – but was that what she wanted?

She didn't understand the chaotic turmoil of her emotions. When he released her wrist, she rubbed the bruised flesh almost absently, and she was still there when Tina came to clear the plates away.

Curried eggs and salad comprised the main course, and Charlotte pushed hers round her plate with a feeling of impatience towards her own indecisiveness. What was wrong with her now? Did she actually gain some enjoyment from these periodic skirmishes with the man who was now her husband? Was she actually sorry that he had withdrawn from the battle?

When the meal was over, Alex rose to his feet. "If you'll excuse me," he said. "Dinner is at eight. No doubt I'll see you then."

Charlotte looked up at him. "Yes," she said, in a small voice, and with a brief nod he left her.

For three days, Charlotte only saw her husband at mealtimes. They were long days, lonely days, when she seldom ventured far from the villa. She ate breakfast in her room, and afterwards either sunbathed on the patio, or went down to the beach to paddle in the sea. She had not swum yet, nor had she encountered her husband again as she had that first morning.

Lunch was invariably at two, and afterwards she rested on the bed with one of the books taken from the library which Maria had taken much delight in showing her. Then afternoon tea was at five, served on the patio, for which Alex did join her, and dinner was at eight. This meal was over by about nine or half past, and although she knew that Alex went into the lounge and listened to music at this time, he never invited her to join him. Consequently, she was in bed by ten most nights, although not always to sleep.

Occasionally she saw Vittorio and Dimitrios about the villa. She had learned from Maria that the Santos brothers lived in the village over the headland, but as Alex was supposed to be taking a holiday, their presence was not often required.

It was, for Charlotte, an almost solitary existence. The words she and Alex exchanged over lunch and dinner could scarcely be termed conversation, and her only speech was with the servants.

Then, on the morning of the fourth day, she had an unexpected visitor. Casually dressed in cotton pants and a halter top, she was sitting on the patio reading when Sophia came to announce that Kyria Eleni Faulkner had arrived and was awaiting her in the *saloni*.

"Kyria Eleni?" Charlotte echoed in confusion, getting up hastily from the padded lounger she had been occupying, dropping the aerosol container of lotion she had been using to prevent her skin from becoming burned. "Who – who is that?"

Sophia's dark eyes were faintly hostile, as usual. "Kyria Eleni? *Ine i yaya*," she exclaimed, as if Charlotte should have known this without asking. "The – grandmother, *ne*?"

"Alex's grandmother," breathed Charlotte, under her breath. Of course. Alex had told her his grandmother lived on the island. But what was she doing here? Now? And where was Alex?

Stopping Sophia as she was turning away, Charlotte asked: "Do you – do you know where – where my husband is?"

"*Ohi, kyria*."

Charlotte, even with her small knowledge of the language, did not need Sophia's shaken head to tell her that she did not.

"Oh, very well," she said shortly, dismissing the girl, and taking a deep breath, walked into the villa.

Eleni Faulkner was an intimidating figure. Tall, taller even than Charlotte, she was not a slim woman, and her ample curves were concealed beneath a long black dress which reached almost to her ankles. It was a curious thing to Charlotte that many Greek women seemed to favour such dark colours in a climate where lighter shades would have deflected the heat. Dark-skinned, like her grandson, Eleni had the distinction of almost white hair, which contrasted sharply with her colouring. Despite the fact that Charlotte estimated her age to somewhere between seventy and eighty, she was not stooped, and there was no trace of weakness in that straight, uncompromising back. Coming into the room out of the brightness outside, Charlotte was put at an immediate disadvantage in that the older woman had plenty of time to appraise her before her eyes adjusted themselves to the light.

"Ah, so you are Charlotte." Eleni Faulkner spoke first, her voice strong and firm. "Why has my grandson not brought you to meet me?"

Charlotte's lips parted. "Er – won't you sit down, Kyria Faulkner?" she invited awkwardly. "I – er – Alex isn't here at the moment."

Eleni regarded her suspiciously for a few moments and then with an indifferent tilt of her head allowed herself to be seated on one of the straight-backed armchairs. "Well?" she said, when she was seated. "You haven't answered my question."

Charlotte glanced round and saw with relief that Maria had come to hover near the doorway. Turning back to her visitor, she said: "Can I offer you some coffee?"

Eleni made an impatient sound with her tongue against the roof of her mouth. "I don't drink coffee," she replied. "Chocolate, yes."

Charlotte shrugged and looked at Maria. "Can we offer Kyria Faulkner chocolate?" she inquired, and at Maria's nod: "For – two, please."

Maria gave her a slightly sympathetic smile and went away, and Charlotte subsided into the chair opposite her visitor. "I don't know where Alex is," she said conversationally, almost as though he had just disappeared within the last few minutes. "I'm sorry he's not here to see you. I'm sure he'll be sorry if he misses you. Perhaps you could come to lunch one day. Or dinner – "

"Do stop blabbering, girl." Clearly, Eleni was not above using her age as an excuse for rudeness. "I didn't ask where my grandson was. Knowing him, he's probably messing about in a boat somewhere. I asked why he had not brought you to see me."

Charlotte made a helpless gesture. "I – we've only been here four days. There really hasn't been time – "

"Nonsense. Alex knows me. He knows I was expecting to meet you. *Akooste*, after I have waited almost twenty years for him to take a wife, is it so unreasonable that I should wish to meet her?"

"Of course not." Charlotte linked her hands between her knees. "It's just that – well, you know how it is."

"No, I do not know how it is. That is why I am asking you."

Eleni wasn't letting her get away with that, and reluctantly Charlotte remembered that Alex had intended to show her the island. No doubt that would have included meeting his grandmother, but she had refused to go with him.

Realizing excuses were getting her precisely nowhere, she said: "I'm sorry. I did not imagine you would be so – interested in me."

Eleni's dark eyes narrowed. "And why not? Why should I not be interested in my new granddaughter?"

"What Charlotte means is that back in England grandparents do not perhaps take such an interest in their grandchildren's affairs."

Alex's unmistakable tones had never been so welcome, and Charlotte glanced round with a deeply drawn sigh to find her husband leaning negligently against the door frame. The fact that he was dressed much as she had seen him that first morning – in shabby shorts, only this time with the doubtful distinction of a short-sleeved shirt hanging loosely from his shoulders – meant less than her intense relief at his appearance. Her eyes encountered his, read their unmistakable censure, and quickly looked away.

Alex came into the room and took his grandmother's hand, raising it to his lips, and Eleni said: "Alexandro!" in gently reproving tones. Then she stared at him searchingly, shaking her head at his lack of attire, and went on: "Alexandro, why have you been keeping yourself aloof from me?"

Alex straightened. "Grandmother, we are newly married," he said mildly. "Were you and my grandfather eager for company on your honeymoon?"

Eleni moved her head from side to side. "That was different. Your grandfather and I were not honeymooning in the bosom of the family, as it were. Alexandro – you promised to come and see me!"

Charlotte listened to this interchange with an acute feeling of discomfort. On the one hand she felt responsible for Alex's tardy behaviour, and on the other she objected to the entirely misleading impression he was allowing his grandmother to acquire. And yet what else could he say? How could he explain to this arrogant old woman that his only reason for making this marriage at all involved a hastily contrived gamble and a latent desire for a son and heir?

Maria arrived with the chocolate Eleni had requested, and finding Alex with the two women, offered to get another cup.

"*Ohi, then pirazi*, Maria," replied Alex, shaking his head, and Charlotte guessed he had refused. He turned once more to his grandmother. "You'll join us for lunch, of course. I'll go and change."

Eleni looked piercingly up at him. "No, Alexandro, I won't stay to lunch today. I did not come here to intrude upon your privacy. I came to meet your wife, and I have." Her eyes flickered over Charlotte. "She's a beautiful creature, I can understand your desire to keep her to yourself. But I expect to see you again – soon, *ne*?"

Charlotte glanced up at her husband, realizing something was expected of her. "Er – please stay," she ventured, not quite knowing what he wanted. "You're very welcome."

"Thank you, my dear, but I know when I am not wanted." Eleni indicated the chocolate which Maria had set on a low table in front of Charlotte. "If I can just have some chocolate,

I'll be on my way."

"Chocolate? Oh, yes. Sorry." Charlotte had almost forgotten the chocolate. She struggled to pour the steaming liquid without spilling any. "Of course."

Eleni frowned up at Alex. "You're looking pale, my boy," she commented, startling Charlotte still further. "And your wife is nervous of me," the old woman added, with wry perception. "What have you been telling her?"

Alex managed a smile, although his eyes remained sombre. "You're imagining things, *yaya*," he told her firmly. "And remarking on someone's nervousness is not likely to put them at their ease."

Eleni shrugged, and took the cup of chocolate Charlotte handed to her. "She's too thin, of course," she went on, changing the subject with confusing speed. "But once babies start coming, that will soon change."

"I hope not," retorted Alex calmly. "I like her just the way she is."

Eleni sipped her chocolate slowly, and Charlotte made an effort to drink hers. As his grandmother had refused his offer to stay to lunch, Alex had not gone to get changed, and for that she was grateful; even though it meant he would probably disappear again the minute his grandmother departed.

At last Eleni got up to leave, and both Charlotte and Alex accompanied her to the door. To Charlotte's surprise and delight, a small cart waited outside drawn by a donkey with his ears poking through the brim of a straw boater. Giving a little exclamation of pleasure, she left her husband and his grandmother to approach the animal, stroking his neck and murmuring to him. Until then, she had not given a thought as to how Eleni must have made the journey across the island. She had seen no cars since her arrival, and as most places were accessible on foot she had naturally assumed there was no means of transport.

Eleni came to join her, climbing up on to the front of the cart where a benchlike seat was made a little more comfortable by the addition of cushions. Alex helped his grandmother up, and she took up the reins and a small whip.

"What's his name?" Charlotte asked, unaware of the sudden warmth in her voice as she spoke to the donkey.

Eleni regarded her strangely. "Pepe," she said at last. "Do you like animals?"

Charlotte nodded eagerly. "I love them. We had a dog once . . ." She hesitated. "After my mother died, there was no one to exercise it when I was away at school." She bit her lip, unconsciously wistful. "Daddy said we had to get rid of it."

Eleni and Alex exchanged glances, and then Eleni flicked the whip. "I must be off. I will see you both in a few days. Do not forget, Alexandro."

The donkey cart rattled away along the track which led to the village, and Charlotte felt suddenly bereft. In spite of the tension involved in speaking with Alex's grandmother, there had been a certain stimulation in the exercise, and now she had gone and things would resume their dull pattern.

Alex turned and walked back into the house, and after a few moments she followed him, wandering along the hall which led to the back of the house. The lounger she had occupied earlier awaited her, her book laid conveniently within arm's reach.

There was no sign of Alex and she guessed he had gone to his room. She had learned, by a process of elimination, that Alex occupied the room several doors along from her own, and the brief glimpse she had had of it had shown her that he did not use his wealth for his own comfort. Compared to the room she slept in, it was almost bare, with a locally woven coverlet on the bed and plain white curtains at the windows. The only rug she had seen had been beside the bed, a simple divan of the type to be found in any department store.

She glanced at her watch. It was barely twelve o'clock and there were two hours to kill until lunch time. She felt sweaty after the tension of her encounter with Alex's grandmother, and she thought with longing of that pool Alex had offered to show her. She wondered where it was and whether she could find it on her own, and then discarded the idea. It was too hot to wander aimlessly about the island, and she had no wish to develop sunstroke to add to all her other worries.

She was hesitating at the doorway to the patio when hard hands on her midriff shifted her firmly aside, and Alex passed her to walk across the sun-bleached tiles. He leant against one of the wide stone pillars which supported the entrance to the villa, and glanced back at her with cool appraising eyes. He had changed his shorts for close-fitting cotton pants, but had discarded his shirt altogether.

"Well?" he said challengingly. "What are you thinking?"

Charlotte stepped out on to the patio. "I was thinking that I'm hot and sticky," she admitted honestly.

"What did you think of Eleni?" he persisted, ignoring the unknowing appeal in her words.

Charlotte shrugged. "She's – very nice."

"But inquisitive."

"I didn't say that."

"No. But she is." Alex looked away from her. "I intended to introduce you the other day, but ..." he shrugged. "I guessed she would come, sooner or later."

"You might have warned me."

"Why?" He looked at her over his shoulder. "I haven't noticed any tendency on your part to indulge in conversation with me."

Charlotte thrust moist palms into her hip pockets. "No – well, maybe I was hasty." She spoke half reluctantly, but something was driving her on. "I – perhaps we should – talk to one another. I mean, how else am I going to – to get used to you?"

Alex turned right round, supporting his back against the column. "Go on."

His expression was faintly derisive, and a certain defensiveness crept into her voice. "Well, wouldn't you rather we behaved like – like civilized people?"

"Indeed." He inclined his head. "But I wonder what has changed your mind? Too many hours spent alone, perhaps? I can hardly believe that you're desperate for *my* company!"

Charlotte pursed her lips. "If you're going to be sarcastic – "

"How the hell do you expect me to be?" he demanded harshly. "You stand there and tell me that perhaps you've been hasty, that perhaps we should talk to one another! Perhaps I don't want to talk to you!"

Charlotte was amazed how easily he could hurt her. Holding up her head, she said: "I wish I'd never mentioned it."

Alex shook his head impatiently. "Oh? Are we now to revert back to our childish tantrums? Are you withdrawing your so-generous offer?"

"You're a brute, do you know that?" she stormed tremulously.

"And you're a sweet misunderstood girl. I know. Forgive me if I find the analogy rather hard to take!"

Charlotte gasped and stalked forward, intending to snatch up her book and leave him, but his fingers round her forearm prevented her.

"Let's stop playing games, shall we?" he suggested, and she was so close to him that his breath mingled with hers. "I'll take you swimming, if that's what you want."

Charlotte's eyes flashed angry indignation and his fingers tightened warningly. "Don't deny it," he admonished quietly. "I might just take you at your word."

Charlotte wrenched herself free, unwilling to admit the disturbing exhilaration these confrontations always aroused inside her. She could still feel the hardness of his hand against her flesh, and she rubbed her arm with impatient fingers. She was fighting a battle inside her, fighting against the impulses which were driving her towards him. But weakness won.

"All right," she got out at last. " – I would like to go swimming."

Alex straightened and walked across the patio, turning his back on her. "You do have a swimsuit, don't you?" he inquired rather flatly, and then: "Get it. You're wasting time."

Charlotte hesitated only a moment longer, and then pressing her balled fists against her thighs, she marched into the house.

In her room, she took off her trousers and halter top and put on one of the half dozen bikinis Verna had insisted she needed. It was all white, two diminutive scraps of cotton that revealed the whiteness of her skin below the waistband of the trousers she normally wore. She put her trousers on again over the bikini brief, but decided the halter top would look rather silly over her bikini bra. Instead, she thrust it into a canvas bag along with a towel.

Alex was waiting for her in the hall, without either towel or trunks as far as she could see, although like her he could be wearing his swimming gear underneath. Her heart quickened automatically.

"Ready?" he inquired coolly, and she nodded, preceding him outside. He took her bag from her unresisting fingers and said: "Come on. Follow me."

It was hot, much hotter now than when Eleni had left in her donkey trap. Following Alex across the rough ground, Charlotte was soon tired, and her legs ached from the unaccustomed exercise. All around them the sea gleamed invitingly, the sound of the water splashing on the rocks below them, a tantalising temptation.

Alex was used to this terrain, and he strode easily ahead, pausing now and then to allow her to catch up. He didn't say anything, but she was glad. She didn't think she would have the breath for conversation as well.

At last he stopped and pointed down what appeared to be a sheer cliff face. "This is it," he said, not attempting to hide his amusement at her hot cheeks. "Come on, take my hand. It's rather steep."

Charlotte allowed her fingers to entwine with his, and gasped when she saw where he was taking her. An overhang of rock concealed a track that was half path, half rocky steps gouged out of the cliff itself. It wound downwards, a haunt for sheep and goats, Charlotte thought wryly, but surely not for man.

Keeping her eyes on Alex's broad back, she allowed him to precede her down the slope, not daring to think what might happen if he slipped. Below them, the water sucked greedily along the base of the cliffs, subsiding in showers of spray which, as they neared the bottom, wet them, too. At last they reached the flat plateau of rock which provided a natural diving platform, and Charlotte could see the curving promontory which formed the pool's basin.

Alex released her hand, and looked at her laughingly. "Do you realize you've nearly broken my fingers?" he asked, flexing them painfully.

Charlotte's tension relaxed into giggles. "I'm sorry, but it was so steep!" She looked back the way they had come and shuddered. "Heavens, do we actually have to go back up there?"

"It's easier going up than coming down, actually," Alex told her reassuringly, kicking off his sandals. "Well? Was it worth it?"

"Mm." Charlotte looked about her excitedly. "I can't wait to get into the water."

"Go ahead!" Alex indicated the pool, and trying not to feel too self-conscious she stripped off her trousers and walked to the edge of the platform.

She dipped her toe first. Against her heated flesh, the water felt cold, but after a few moments she became more daring and sat down to dangle her feet in the water. She was aware that Alex had seated himself further back on the shelf of rock, his back against the cliff, one leg drawn up to support his elbow.

Deciding it was now or never, Charlotte slipped off the

platform, allowing herself to submerge slowly beneath the waves, opening her eyes on a green-shrouded world of rocks and waving seaweed.

When she came up again to take some air, she was near the middle of the pool, and Alex was standing on the edge of the platform, his eyes showing the anxiety he had obviously experienced. She swam back to him, shaking the hair out of her eyes, wanting to reassure him. "Were you worried about me?" she exclaimed.

"What do you think?" he demanded roughly. Then, more calmly: "How is it?"

"Marvellous!" she replied, turning on to her back and floating, closing her eyes against the glare of the sun. "Aren't you coming in?"

Alex shook his head. "I think not."

She came upright, eyes wide again. "Why not? Aren't you hot?"

"Mmm," he nodded. "But ..." He paused. "Enjoy yourself!" And he walked back to his earlier position on the platform.

Charlotte rested her arms and her chin on the shelf, regarding him steadily. "What is it? I thought we'd agreed to call a truce."

"We have. And I don't want to start hostilities again." Then as she still continued to look puzzled, he said: "Charlotte, I haven't swum in trunks since I was eight years old!"

"Oh!" Charlotte turned abruptly away and swam swiftly across the pool. She should have guessed. What reason would he have for wearing anything here? This was his island, this pool was probably private property. And that would account for his tan which did not appear to be confined to any particular area of his body. It was a curiously disturbing idea, and she was glad of the water to hide the sudden wave of heat which swept all over her body.

Even so, it was lonely swimming alone. She wished he could

have joined her. No doubt he would, if she asked him to, but...

She swam back to the side, and wrinkling her nose said: "Who else swims here?"

Alex shrugged. He had taken out a case of cheroots and was lighting one. He inhaled deeply before replying: "No one but me these days. When I was a child I used to swim with Vittorio and Dimitrios and some of the other boys, but nowadays..." He shrugged expressively.

Charlotte nodded. "What time is it?"

He consulted his watch. "Quarter past one."

"What time do we have to leave?"

"Fifteen, maybe twenty minutes."

"Oh." Charlotte nodded again and looked back at the water. "I don't suppose I would dare to come here alone – "

"Don't even think about it!" said Alex harshly. "It can be dangerous, swimming in deep water. If you got cramp..."

"I know."

Charlotte gave a wistful little sigh and letting go of the rock swam lazily across the pool again. She was turning to swim back when something struck the centre of the pool, something sleek and dark and powerful, something that caused very little spray as it entered the water. It all happened too quickly for her to feel any fear, and when Alex's dark head emerged only a few feet away from her, she felt only relief that he had decided to join her after all.

His smile was faintly self-derisory, however, as he said: "I'll promise not to take advantage of you, if you'll promise the same," and she smiled. "You did want me to join you, didn't you?" he added.

Charlotte nodded. "Yes. Oh, yes."

The next half hour flew on freedom's wings. Charlotte had never indulged in water sports before, but Alex soon had her swimming and diving and racing, enjoying the elemental release of it all. He was an expert swimmer and she knew he tempered his speed to her breathless efforts. He taught her how to hold her breath for longer periods of time, how to control her breathing, swimming with her to the break in the rock wall where the sea spilled through into the underwater caverns he had explored as a boy.

But eventually they had to leave the water, and Alex hung back while Charlotte towelled herself dry and put on her trousers over the bikini. She left the halter top in the bag, the heat of the sun already drying the bra of the bikini against her skin. She averted her eyes as Alex vaulted out and borrowed her towel to dry himself. Curiously enough, she felt no real embarrassment any more. After all, she thought, this man is my husband! And then was shocked at the realization that she was coming to accept the situation.

They saw Maria looking out for them as they approached the villa. Her gnarled features revealed her concern, and Charlotte guessed she had been worried about them. She said something reproving to Alex in her own language, and then, when he insisted: "English, Maria!" she went on: "Where have you been? It is long after two o'clock! I was about to send Sophia to the village for Vittorio!"

Alex patted the old woman's shoulder affectionately. "We've been swimming, Maria, and I guess we forgot the time."

"Swimming?" Maria's dark eyes flickered over Charlotte's flushed skin and tangled hair. "Ah – ah, yes, I see."

Charlotte understood only too well what the old woman thought she saw, and now she was embarrassed. Naturally Maria would know of Alex's swimming habits and imagined no doubt some tender love scene down there beside the pool. With a toss of her head, she brushed past both of them, and went into the villa.

CHAPTER FIVE

When Charlotte appeared for lunch, Alex was waiting for her at the table. He had put on a shirt and combed his straight hair, but that was all. Charlotte meanwhile had showered and changed into a white poplin shift that left her arms and most of her legs exposed to the sun.

After she was seated and Tina had served them each with a bowl of iced consommé, Alex spoke. "These past couple of hours," he said slowly. "Did you enjoy yourself?"

Charlotte decided to be honest. "Very much."

"Then don't you think it would be more sensible if we spent more time together?" he suggested quietly.

Charlotte looked up and found his dark eyes upon her. She looked away again. "What does that mean exactly?"

Alex's grimace was exasperated. "Well, it doesn't mean in bed, if that's what you're afraid of!"

Charlotte spooned soup into her mouth. "Is that what you want?" she asked tentatively.

Alex sighed. "Yes. I see no reason why we shouldn't be – friends, at least."

"How can I be your friend?" Charlotte exclaimed, feeling almost a traitor at the thought.

"How can you be my enemy?" he retorted, and with an exclamation of impatience got up from the table and walked to the top of the shallow stairs which led down into the hall. Then he turned to look at her, his hands in his pockets, the close-fitting pants exposing the taut muscles of his thighs. "Charlotte, I've been very patient with you, more patient than you could have expected me to be. Why do you continue to fight me every inch of the way? Is your life here so miserable? Is it such an arduous existence I've chosen for you?

Would you rather be in the chills and fogs of an approaching English winter?"

Charlotte put down her spoon. "Those are not fair questions."

"I disagree. You're here, aren't you? And you are my wife. How many times must I remind you of that?"

"I don't need reminding," she retorted, pushing back the heavy swathe of hair which fell across her cheek. Then despising herself because of it, she added: "Come and eat your lunch. You must be hungry."

Alex's eyes narrowed. "What do you care? You'd stand by and see me starve! Don't deny it."

"But I do," she protested fiercely. "I – I wouldn't stand by and see anybody starve!"

"Oh, thanks very much."

Alex resumed his seat, his expression sardonic, and with a feeling of remorse, she exclaimed: "All right, all right. Let's – try it. Spending more time together, I mean."

Alex frowned. "Is this some new gambit?" he asked suspiciously.

Charlotte had to smile. "No. No, I mean it. You can – show me the island. I really would like to see all of it."

During the next few days, Charlotte ignored her conscience and allowed herself to enjoy Alex's company. And he was good company. He knew the contours of the island blindfold, from the wilder coastline at the north side of the island to the sunbleached coves below the villa. The barren cliffs made the island a virtual fortress, and it came as no surprise to her to learn that that was why Alex's father had acquired it. His subsequent death at the hands of terrorist assassins made his vulnerability that much more real, and Charlotte found herself wondering whether Alex ever thought about the dangers he ran when he left the island. He had a bodyguard, of course, but what good would he be in the face of machine-gun bullets?

They went swimming, Alex subjugating his love of freedom for her benefit by wearing his shorts in the water. He taught her how to handle the power launch which took them swiftly out into the blue-green waters of the Aegean, and twice he took her sailing in the bay. The first occasion, he took her in the racing dinghy she had seen that first morning. Charlotte had only rarely crewed for her father, and in spite of the poignancy of that remembrance, she found it an exhilarating experience. On the second occasion, they used the twin-hulled catamaran which she soon learned was his real obsession. It occupied pride of place in the boathouse, alongside the launch, and had the quixotic name of *Easy Rider*.

Unlike her father, Alex did not insist on handling everything himself. He was quite prepared to give her control for a while, and with him stretched out lazily on the cabin roof, she felt the certain thrill of complete possession. It was at times like these when she found it almost impossible to drum up any feeling of antagonism towards him.

As well as showing her the island, Alex talked to her. He knew the islands of the Cyclades like the back of his hand – their people, their industry, their legends. Charlotte found the legends particularly fascinating. She had always loved the magic that could be found in myths and fairy stories, and when she discovered accidentally from Maria that Lydros had its own legend she was eager to hear it.

But in this Alex proved strangely reticent, and it was left to her to search among the books in the library until she found what she was looking for. She was curled up in an armchair after dinner one evening, studying a massive tome of myths and legends she had taken from the shelf, when Alex came into the library.

She was surprised to see him. The strains of a Carpenters L.P. drifted through from the lounge, and she had thought he was in there, listening to it. These past few days she had learned that he liked all kinds of music, from beat music and jazz to the classical composers, and the similarities in their tastes had been quite startling. But now he strolled into the room, dark and disturbing, in close-fitting black pants and a dark red silk shirt.

"What are you doing?" he asked, squinting at the ledgerlike volume she was supporting on her culotte-clad knees. "What is it? Myths and legends?"

She looked up. "I'm looking for the Lydros legend," she told him levelly. "You don't have any objections, do you?"

Alex lifted the huge book out of her hands. "As a matter of fact, yes."

Charlotte screwed up her face disappointedly. "Oh, don't take it away," she pleaded. "I'd just found it."

Alex closed the book with a distinct thud. "Why are you so curious about our legend?" he demanded.

"Why shouldn't I be?" she protested, getting out of her chair, slim and youthful in the vivid blending of blues and greens to be found in her culotte suit. She stretched out her hand to take the book again. "Alex, please! Don't be mean!"

He smiled then, a lazy teasing smile, that did strange things to her lower limbs, so that despising the weakness, she flopped down into her chair again. Her lips curved sulkily, and Alex regarded her with knowing amusement.

"All right," he said at last, and her eyes widened. "If you're so determined to hear it, I'll tell you. It's quite simple really. Lydros – that was the god's name, of course – rescued a beautiful maiden from the wreck of a vessel come to grief on the rocks around our coastline." He paused. "Lydros fell in love with the girl, but she thought he was old and ugly, and she was terrified of him. But he made her live on the island, and gradually, over a period of time, she came to know him and care for him. He didn't know this, until he finally took pity on her and offered to send her away, and she refused to go. That's all there is to it."

"Oh, I like it!" Charlotte had been listening intently, and now she leaned forward, her chin cupped in her hands. "It's almost like the story of Beauty and the Beast, isn't it?" she breathed. "Except that the girl's father wasn't involved. Oh – "

She broke off suddenly and stared at him, and Alex's mouth turned down at the corners. He turned away and thrust the book back into its place on the shelves. "Beware the Beast!" he remarked mockingly, and left the room.

Charlotte turned to stare after him, her brow furrowed. Now she knew why he had not wanted her to read the story. There were too many similarities to her own situation. She turned back, and grimaced at her hands. But Alex was not old – or ugly – and she was no longer afraid of him.

Pressing her hands down on the arms of her chair, she got to her feet again, and padded slowly through to the lounge. Alex was standing by the drinks trolley, helping himself to a large scotch. Even as she watched, he threw the raw spirit to the back of his throat, wincing slightly at the onslaught. Then he seemed to sense that he was not alone, for he half turned and saw her in the doorway. He frowned down at his empty glass for a moment, and then with a shrug replaced it on the tray.

"Well?" he said. "Have you finished reading for this evening?"

Charlotte nodded. "Alex, I – I want you to know, I had no idea . . . "

His lips twisted. "No idea about what?"

"Oh, you know what I mean! The legend, that story!"

"What about it?"

His eyes were narrowed and challenging and she sighed impatiently. "Alex, you know what I'm trying to say. You're not making it very easy for me."

He ran a hand over his thick hair, coming to rest at the back of his neck. Then he gestured with his free hand towards the trolley. "Can I offer you a drink?"

Charlotte scuffed her bare toe against a skin rug. "No. I'm not thirsty."

"Are you going to sit down, then?" he suggested, indicating a nearby couch.

"Why won't you talk about it?" she burst out at length as he walked over to the turntable to change the record. "I know you think there are comparisons to our situation, but it's not really similar. I mean – well, I'm not afraid of you."

Alex straightened and looked at her. "Aren't you?" he asked quietly.

"No." Charlotte took a deep breath. "And you're not old, or – or ugly."

Alex half smiled then. "Oh, yes, Charlotte, I am old. At least old enough to be your father."

She flushed. "Age has nothing to do with it. You're not like – like Daddy was." She bent her head, realizing what she was saying. She, who had maintained she would always hate this man. "I suppose I seem childish to you, but that doesn't mean you're old!"

Alex bent to set the automatic player in motion, and presently the strings of the bouzouki filled the room with their plaintive melody. Then he turned back to her and smiled. "Come on, I'll teach you how to dance to this music. Do you want to learn?"

Charlotte looked at him mutinously through her lashes. "Oh – oh, all right," she conceded with ill grace, and he came towards her, smiling at her frustration.

Charlotte had seen Greek dancing before, on television, but that had not prepared her for the reality. Alex's arm about her shoulders brought her close beside him, its weight a distracting influence to the things he was attempting to teach her. Her own arm was around his waist and she was conscious that only the fine material of his shirt separated her from the muscular warmth of his hard body.

Even so, she tried to concentrate on what he was saying, following the sideways movements without too much difficulty, the crossing steps – three times, twice, once, dip. The music on the turntable was gradually quickening, and their steps quickened in time to the music. Charlotte forgot her awareness of her husband in the simple concentration of the dance. Her breathing had quickened, and she emitted little gasps of achievement as she managed to keep up with him. She was laughing up into his face, confident of her own ability, when she missed a step and gasped with pain as Alex's suede-booted foot came down on her bare toes. She crumpled away from him, sinking down on to the floor to nurse her bruised toes, and he came down on his haunches beside her, his face taut with anxiety.

"God, I'm sorry," he muttered, brushing her hands aside and taking the injured foot between his own fingers. "Does it hurt a lot?"

Charlotte raised half humorous eyes to his. "Mmm," she admitted teasingly. "You're no light weight, you know."

His expression softened. "Well, I don't think there are any bones broken anyway. Can you stand, or shall I lift you?"

Charlotte shook her head, resenting a little his concern for her, which smacked of patronage. "I can manage." She struggled to her feet, resisting his assistance. "The pain's wearing off now. I'm not a child, you know, to be picked up every time it hurts itself!"

Alex looked at her with curiously intent eyes. "I never imagined you were."

"No, but you do think of me as a child, don't you?" she exclaimed. "Talking about being old enough to be my father!"

Alex's eyes darkened. "How would you have me behave? You want I should treat you as a woman? As my wife?"

Charlotte coloured hotly. "I – I just want to be treated as an adult, that's all."

Alex turned away, his jaw taut with impatience. "This is a stupid conversation!" he told her flatly. "I married you, didn't I?"

"I sometimes wonder why!" she flashed, almost without thinking, and he turned on her angrily.

"Oh, Charlotte! Don't provoke me! We're only just beginning to have some kind of a relationship. Don't imagine anything has changed!"

Charlotte's breasts heaved. "Oh, I see. So – so these past days, they've just been pretence, have they?"

"*No!*" Alex smote his fist against his thigh. "No. They've been – ordinary, satisfactory days, when we've enjoyed each other's company. Or at least, I've enjoyed yours. You may not have enjoyed mine, but there's nothing I can do about that!"

Charlotte hunched her shoulders, feeling ridiculously near to tears. They had been good days, and now she was coming dangerously near to ruining them.

"I – I do enjoy your company," she murmured unhappily. "Oh, Alex, I'm sorry. I was just being – bitchy."

He expelled his breath on a heavy sigh. "Yes – well, let's forget it, shall we?"

Charlotte stretched out a hand and touched his arm, bare to the elbow where he had rolled back his sleeves. She could feel the taut muscles, sense his instinctive stiffening without actually seeing it. "Alex, don't be mad at me! I know I say the wrong things – *do* the wrong things. But I don't like it when you – patronize me."

"Patronize you?" He raised his eyes heavenwards. "I don't patronize you, Charlotte. Oh, for God's sake – " He put his free hand over hers, holding it against his arm, and her pulses raced alarmingly at this exhibition of how easily he could take control of her emotions. His eyes held hers captive, and there was a caressing quality about them which weakened her knees and set her trembling. "Charlotte, believe me, I do not regard you as a child. God forgive me, perhaps I should, but I don't."

Charlotte found it incredibly difficult to articulate at all. "I – I – it's getting late. I – I'm tired," she managed jerkily, and to her relief, he allowed her to withdraw her fingers. "Good – goodnight, Alex."

He made no reply, merely nodded his head, and the sudden

gauntness of his expression was almost her undoing. She realized with a shattering sense of horror at her own body's duplicity that had he drawn her into his arms just then, she would not have been able – or wanted – to stop him.

In the bedroom, she stared at her reflection with troubled eyes. The colour in her cheeks was hectic, her eyes were abnormally bright, and her breathing was more rapid than could be accounted for by merely walking along the length of the corridor. Her feet were still bare, and she remembered she had left her cork-soled sandals in the library. Thinking of the library reminded her once more of the legend, but with a brisk determination she refused to think of that, and went quickly into the bathroom.

But once she was in bed, between the satin sheets, her thoughts were not so easy to control, and she despised herself for the way she had behaved. Was she so impressionable that two weeks of Alex's company could make her completely forget her reasons for being there? Was his personality such that she had no control over her own feelings? Could she excuse so easily his determination to make her honour her father's debt? She refused to acknowledge such things, and with a smothered gulp buried her face in the lace-covered pillow.

She awoke in the pale light of dawn to the realization that someone was sitting on the side of the bed, gently shaking her. She opened her eyes reluctantly, and widened them in amazement when she recognized Alex's shadowy frame.

"What do you want?"

Alex was partially dressed, and as her eyes adjusted themselves to the light, she realized his trousers were dark and immaculately creased, and his unbuttoned shirt was made of white silk. They were not at all the sort of clothes he had worn about the island, and a twinge of alarm feathered along her veins.

"I have to leave," he told her quietly. "Within the next

hour. I've had word from the States that there's some hang-up over the Achilles merger. It must be pretty important or they wouldn't have had George contact me. He's waiting in the salon. He came in the helicopter, and we'll take it back to Athens and fly out from there in the jet. With a bit of luck we should be in New York by this afternoon, their time."

Charlotte absorbed this with dismay. Propping herself up on her elbows, uncaring right then that the sheet had fallen back to reveal the lace bodice of her nightgown, she stared at him anxiously.

"But couldn't George handle it himself?" she protested. "I mean, this is supposed to be your honeymoon."

"I know." Alex nodded resignedly. "Like I said, it must be important or they wouldn't have contacted me."

Charlotte made an impatient sound. "If you weren't available, they would have had to manage without you."

"But I am available," he pointed out steadily, running a questing hand over the hair on his chest. "Honey, I'm sorry."

"So am I." Charlotte chewed worriedly at her lower lip. As she became fully alert, other anxieties were troubling her. His own father had been killed by a terrorist's bullet, and yet he was taking leaving the island so calmly. To her, it had become a retreat, and the world outside had ceased to exist.

"Alex . . ." She stretched out her hand and touched his chest, her nails digging into his flesh. "Alex, I don't want you to go."

She heard his swiftly in-drawn breath, as he said roughly: "Do you think I want to leave you?"

Her fingers strayed slowly up to his chin, and with a surge of emotion, she cupped his cheek. "Oh, Alex, there are men out there who probably hate you just as much as they hated your father!"

Alex turned his head so that his mouth encountered her palm. "I don't think about things like that," he muttered huskily.

"But you should!" she breathed, suddenly achingly aware of her own vulnerability so far as he was concerned. "Alex, don't go!"

"I must," he said harshly. "I have no choice."

"Then let me come with you."

"No."

His refusal brooked no argument, and Charlotte's lips trembled. With an exclamation, almost of impatience, his hand slid down her bare arm to her shoulder, sliding the strap of her nightgown aside so that he could bend his head and touch the soft skin he had exposed with caressing lips. He smelt of shaving lotion and soap after his shower, and his hair was still damp where it brushed her cheek. The dark hair on his chest was rough against the creamy skin rising from the lowcut bodice of her nightgown, but it was not an unpleasant roughness. Charlotte's breathing was laboured and shallow, but when his mouth moved over her throat and cheek to hers, she expelled a small sigh of involuntary satisfaction. Her arms slid round his neck, under the fine material of his shirt, and with an urgency that was taking possession of her, too, Alex shrugged off the shirt without taking his mouth from hers. Then he gathered her completely into his arms, and buried his face in the silky tangle of her hair.

"Your trousers!" she protested, desperately trying to hold on to sanity. "They'll be ruined – "

"To hell with them!" he muttered against her neck, and grasping her face brought her mouth to his again.

Whatever kind of life Alex had been living, he was no novice when it came to making love. Charlotte acknowledged this with one small corner of her mind even while the devastating hunger of his kisses drained away the will to resist him. His lips plundered hers passionately, bringing her to an awareness that he was lying beside her on the bed, his body hard and heavy as it moved over hers.

With a groan of impatience, he kicked the covers aside and it was then she realised he had shed the offending trousers and only her nightgown provided a frail barrier between them.

That was when Charlotte began to panic. It started deep inside her, a vague fluttering in her stomach which gradually spread until it engulfed her in a shuddering sense of fear. She moved desperately under him then, dragging her mouth away from his and twisting her face from side to side, gasping: "No! No! You can't – you can't!"

He grasped a handful of her hair, holding her head still, and his features were strained in the pale light. "I don't want to hurt you, Charlotte, but I don't think I can help it! Oh *God,* I want you."

Charlotte's struggles were to no avail. She had driven him beyond the point of no return, and she sobbed against his chest when he tore the nightgown from her. It was an agonising experience, and only his mouth silenced the scream that rose in her throat as he took her. Then it was all over and he got up from the bed while she buried her face in the pillows.

She heard him moving about, dressing probably, but refused to look at him. She felt degraded and humiliated, and she couldn't bear to see the satisfaction in his face. How could anyone suffer such indignities for pleasure? she asked herself bitterly. Dear God, what had she let herself in for?

"I've got to go, Charlotte." Alex's voice was harsh in the stillness, but she didn't look round. "Charlotte, for God's sake, what do you want me to say?"

"Nothing!" she mumbled into the pillow, and gasped when he caught her arms and flung her on to her back.

He was dressed now, his shirt buttoned almost to the top, dark and disturbingly attractive, and she hated him for it. With trembling fingers, she dragged the covers over her limbs, while he looked down at her coldly.

"Can't you at least say goodbye to your husband?" he demanded.

Charlotte gulped. "Yes, yes. Goodbye. Just go!"

"Is that all?"

"I should ask you that!" she retorted bitterly.

"Charlotte, you were a virgin! There was no way to make it easy for you."

"I don't want to talk about it. If that's all there is to it, then I don't even want to think about it." She shuddered.

Alex sighed frustratedly. "Charlotte, if I had the time I would show you how much better it can be – "

"No, you wouldn't!" she replied stormily. "Don't you dare touch me again!"

"Oh, *God!*" Alex raked a hand through his hair, staring at her with angry eyes. "This is some way to send me on my trip, isn't it?"

"You can't blame me for that." Charlotte sniffed. "Why don't you go? *Go!* George will be getting impatient. Go and tell him what you've done!"

"Charlotte, I warn you – " He broke off, his expression violent. "All right. All right, I'm going. I'll let you know when I'll be back."

"Don't bother!" Charlotte retorted coldly, and buried her face in the pillow again.

She didn't see him go. She heard the helicopter rise over the villa and presently fade into the distance, and only then did the hot tears flood down over her pale cheeks.

CHAPTER SIX

In spite of her distress, Charlotte must have fallen asleep again because she awakened to the sound of Tina saying her name over and over. She opened her eyes reluctantly, aware of a curious aching sensation in her lower limbs which at once resolved itself into a bitter remembrance of what had occurred. She was also made aware of her nakedness beneath the thin satin sheet, and a wave of embarrassment swept over her. The Greek girl was standing beside the bed, and although it was a futile exercise at this late stage, Charlotte rolled over on to her stomach, turning her head sideways on the pillow and saying rather resentfully: "What do you want?"

Tina's sharp eyes had missed nothing of the tumbled state of the bedcovers and Charlotte's discomfort, but her voice was gentle as she replied: "Maria was worried, *kyria*. Is eleven o'clock!"

"Eleven o'clock!" Charlotte echoed her words disbelievingly, but she propped herself up on her elbows and reaching for her watch from the bedside table saw in dismay that it was indeed ten minutes past eleven.

"Kyrios Alexandros left very early this morning, didn't he, *kyria*?" Tina went on conversationally, in a sympathetic tone. "What a pity, *ohi*?"

Charlotte hunched her slim shoulders, feeling the sheet slipping away but hardly caring. Her throat was tightening, and tears were not far away. "It doesn't matter," she managed in a cold little voice. Then: "Tell Maria I'm sorry she was worried. I'll get up right away."

"No hurry, *kyria*," exclaimed Tina at once. "So long as you are not ill . . ."

"I'm not ill," retorted Charlotte crossly. "You can go now. Tell Maria I don't want any breakfast."

"Oh, but *kyria* – "

"Nothing," Charlotte insisted, meeting the other girl's eyes squarely, and muttering resignedly to herself, Tina went away.

After she had gone, Charlotte got out of bed. Her reflection in the long mirrors of the wardrobe caught her attention, and momentarily she halted, staring at her naked body without pleasure. There ought to be some sign, she thought, some evidence of what had occurred, but there was none. The slim lines of her body looked exactly as usual, the flesh turning honey gold in places, contrasting with the paler skin hidden from the sun by her pants or bikini. Discolorations of her flesh in places revealed themselves as bruising, and her lips trembled. Clenching her fists, she turned away and walked into the bathroom. She took a bath as hot as she could stand it, a ridiculous affectation in this heat, and scrubbed violently at her skin as if she could erase the touch of Alex's hard, demanding hands.

She emerged from her room in time for lunch, and although she had no appetite, she made an effort to eat the food which Cristof had so delicately prepared. Stuffed eggs and savoury sausages, a light cheese pie served with salad, a caramel custard that melted in the mouth, Charlotte had a little of each, and realized with increasing bitterness that her lack of appetite would probably be attributed to Alex's abrupt departure. Tina was bound to have gossiped about what she had seen in the bedroom, and Charlotte's vain attempt at concealment had seemed stupid when she found her torn nightgown lying on the floor in a place where Tina could not have failed to see it.

Sighing heavily, Charlotte left the table and walked down the shallow steps to the hall. Pausing by the open doors, she stared out broodingly towards the curving headland. She was virtually a prisoner here, she thought, emotion arousing a kind of panic inside her. If only they had been near a town, civilization of any sort, she could have left the villa, escaped the inevitable feeling of speculation, sought someone to talk to. As it was, she was confined to Maria and the other servants, and they would never understand the way she was feeling right now.

In truth, she didn't altogether understand how she felt herself. She felt shocked and bitter, unwilling even to contemplate that ghastly thing that had happened to her, her legs weakening every time she allowed its implications to creep into her mind. There were even times when she wished that Alex was here so that she might expunge some of her anger and resentment on him, vent her frustration and contempt that he should have violated her in such a way. But mostly, she dreaded the very idea of seeing him again, of living in fear that he might touch her as he had touched her in the early hours of this morning.

For the rest of that strangely unreal day, she paced the rooms and corridors of the villa, unable to settle to anything, even reading, walking and thinking and coming up with nothing except her own utter desolation. How could she have allowed herself to like him, to actually admit to caring about what happened to him? As all the details of what had happened came to light, she had to admit that in some small way she had invited what had happened. And that was the bitterest thing of all to bear.

The following afternoon, a note arrived at the villa. It was delivered by hand and addressed to Charlotte, and she was not altogether surprised to discover it was from Alex's grandmother. The note was brief and to the point. She was invited to lunch the next day. Yanni, the elderly man who had brought the note, would come for her at noon, in the donkey cart.

It was more than an invitation. It was a summons. And Charlotte could think of no reasonable excuse she could give for refusing. Nevertheless, she accepted the invitation with some misgivings, remembering the old woman's penetrating stare and dominating manner. Somehow, between now and then, she would have to marshall some sense of composure so that Eleni Faulkner should not guess at the events which had occurred since their last meeting.

But before her visit to Alex's grandmother's house, there was another message for her. It came via the helicopter, and when Charlotte heard the machine's powerful engines low over the villa, all tenuous calmness left her. This morning she had risen early, and had asked that her breakfast be served in the dining area, but now, hearing those engines, convinced that Alex had returned unexpectedly, she wished she had remained in the comparative safety of her room.

She heard the excited chatter of the women's voices as the helicopter landed. No doubt they were surprised that she did not rise and go to meet her husband, but her legs felt like jellies, and she remained frozen in her chair.

Presently, a man's voice could be heard, interjected amongst the higher tones of the women, speaking in fluent Greek. It was a voice Charlotte had heard before, but it was not Alex's, and her hands relaxed their grip on the edge of the table. Maria appeared in the hall below, and behind her came George Constandis. He appeared to be alone, as Maria gestured upward, and that brought Charlotte out of her seat to stand nervously waiting while he mounted the steps to her level.

"*Kalimera, kyria,*" he spoke politely, with a half bow. "You are well?"

"*Kalimera.*" Charlotte used the Greek word of greeting automatically. Then, jerkily: "Where – where is he?"

"He? You mean Alex?" George halted at the other side of of the table. "He is not here. He is in New York – as you know."

Charlotte's brow furrowed. "But you – aren't you supposed to be in New York, too? You were going with him."

"Our plans were changed when we reached Athens. It was arranged that Alex should fly on to New York – "

"*Alone?*" Charlotte's interruption was almost an accusation, and George smiled.

"There is no need for alarm, *kyria.* Alex is never alone. Dimitrios is with him, naturally."

Charlotte despised herself for the way she had reacted, but, she told herself impatiently, she would feel the same about anyone taking unnecessary risks.

"All I meant was – I'm surprised he can manage without you," she retorted hastily, frustrated by the knowing look in his eyes.

"Well, as I was saying," he went on, "our plans were changed. It was agreed that I should remain in Athens until Alex telephoned me his intentions."

Charlotte sat down again, crumbling the roll on her plate. "And now he has?" she prompted coldly.

"Yes." George nodded. "I am to tell you that something most unfortunate has happened." Charlotte's head jerked up, and he continued: "The man, Steiner, who was handling the merger we have been negotiating, has been rushed to hospital with a suspected rupture of the spleen. This is a most unhappy state of affairs, *kyria.* The point being that apart from Steiner, only Alex himself can interpret all the details of the merger. Consequently . . ." he shrugged, "Alex must stay on in New York until the deal is settled."

Charlotte sagged against the table. She did not know exactly what she had been expecting, but not this. Her brain could not handle the confusion of emotions George Constandis's news had aroused within her, and she found herself staring at him without actually seeing him.

Pulling herself together, she made an effort to behave normally. "I . . . I see." She licked her dry lips. "Er . . . won't you sit down, Mr. Constandis?" She picked up the bell and rang it. "Tina will bring us some fresh coffee."

"Thank you." George seated himself in the chair Alex usually occupied. "I am sorry to be the bearer of bad news."

Charlotte made a gesture of indifference as the Greek girl appeared from the kitchen. She ordered coffee for her guest, and then applied herself to finishing her own breakfast. But it was impossible to feel any enthusiasm for eating when her brain and stomach churned unmercifully.

Tina brought fresh rolls with the coffee, smiling confidently at George Canstandis. He teased her, asking her about her boy-friends, and sending her away giggling. It was obvious he was quite at home here, and although Charlotte had no reason to resent it, she found herself doing so. It was ridiculous, but she resented his coming here, she resented his easy sympathy, his camaraderie with the servants, and most of all his assumption that she was missing her husband. She was tempted to tell him that so far as she was concerned, if Alex chose to spend the next six months in New York, she wouldn't care. But that would have been childish, and not completely true. She wanted this charade over and done with, and how could it be so if he was thousands of miles away? So she bit her tongue, and answered him in monosyllables when he asked what she thought of the island.

At last the meal was over and he rose to his feet. "Thank you, that was delightful," he told her, which Charlotte thought could not be completely true either in the circumstances. "And now, I must leave you."

With reluctance, she found herself unable to deny the obvious question: "I – will you – are you going to New York, too?"

George regarded her steadily. "I am. Why? Do you have a message for your husband? A letter, perhaps?"

"No." Charlotte took a deep breath. "No message."

George hesitated. "You are sure?"

"Quite sure." Charlotte rose too.

He inclined his head. "Very well, *kyria*." He moved towards the steps. "No doubt your husband will keep you informed of further developments as they occur."

Charlotte's fingers curled round the edge of the table again.

"How long – that is – does Alex expect to be away – very long?"

George shrugged, and spread his hands in continental fashion. "In this case – three, maybe four weeks. Who can say? It depends how far Steiner has reached in his negotiations."

"And this merger is important?"

"Oh, yes, *kyria.*"

"But why? What is it for?" Charlotte couldn't prevent the sudden outburst. "Doesn't he have enough money?"

"Mergers do not always make money," George corrected her. "At least, not in the way you mean. This particular negotiation will make something far more important. It will make work for a greater number of people."

"Work?"

"Yes, work – jobs. This firm in New York – it is – how do you say it– floundering, *ne*?"

"Why would Alex want to merge with a firm that is floundering?" Charlotte was confused.

George was patient. "With a difficult economic situation, many companies are floundering. But in this instance, there are valuable importing and exporting sanctions which we can use."

"So the people who work for this company won't lose their jobs."

"That is correct."

Charlotte sighed. "I wouldn't have thought Alex would care, one way or the other," she murmured bitterly.

George caught his breath. "Your husband does care. He cares deeply for anyone in difficult circumstances. Why do you think he has so many enemies? Because he inspires a degree of loyalty in his employees which many men could wish to emulate!"

Charlotte flushed at this impassioned outburst, feeling obliged to defend herself. "I know very little about my – my husband's business affairs, or the strength of devotion of his

employees. I only know that so far as I am concerned – "
She broke off abruptly. Not even to this man could she confide her own miserable circumstances.

"*Kyria.*" George was speaking again, leaning towards her, his hands resting on the table. "When your husband's father was killed, the shares in the Faulkner corporation fell dramatically. It was understandable. Steven Faulkner was a brilliant man, a man at the height of his power. Alex was what? Twenty-three, twenty-four? Hardly more than a boy. A trained economist, but that was all. Yet in fifteen years, Alex has not only equalled his father's record, he has overtaken it, and in doing so has won the respect of every professional in the business! We used to be a shipping company – now we have interests in hotels and airlines, travel agencies, oil wells, newspapers. . . . Do you have any idea how many people we keep in employment?"

"Oh, no – *no!*" Charlotte wrapped her arms about herself tightly. "I've told you, I know next to nothing about Alex's affairs. They're nothing to do with me."

"Then perhaps you should make them so," snapped George coldly, and Charlotte's eyes widened in indignation. "I'm sorry," he added, less aggressively, shaking his head. "But I used to work for Steven Faulkner. I was with him the day he died. I followed him out of the hotel in Paris on the day he was shot. I've never forgiven myself for not being first out of that hotel, and consequently my feelings for Alex are as close as any father for his son."

Charlotte stared at him, realizing he meant every word he said. But how could she explain to this man her position? How could she tell him that there was little point in her involving herself with the Faulkner corporation when in – what? – a year, eighteen months? – she would be a free woman again? She simply wasn't interested – was she?

Choosing the least provocative thing so far as she was concerned, she said awkwardly: "You can't really blame yourself for Alex's father's death. I mean, even if you had been first out of the hotel, surely whoever killed Mr. Faulkner would know who he was aiming for?"

George nodded heavily. "Oh yes, I tell myself this, of course. Alex tells me this. But one cannot completely erase the doubts. That is why I urge you not to minimize the risks your husband is running, why you must not behave childishly because you cannot always have your own way."

"My own way?" echoed Charlotte confusedly. "What are you talking about?"

"*Kyria*, life is too short to be small-minded. Refusing to write your husband a letter, refusing him even a kind message! I know you are angry with him. Perhaps you would rather he was here than me. I would rather that myself. But it is not possible. I should add that Alex's mother went everywhere with her husband. Perhaps you should think along those lines yourself!"

"Now wait a minute!"

Charlotte could not allow him to get away with that, but already he had turned and was walking down the steps. Maria's appearance forestalled the retort Charlotte longed to make, and gripping her arms tightly, she followed them across the hall and down the corridor towards the patio.

Another man was waiting outside the villa, seated at a glass-topped table, drinking beer and chatting with Sophia and Tina. They all stood around awkwardly when Charlotte appeared.

"This is Manuelo," George introduced the pilot casually, and Charlotte managed a tight smile at the young Greek in his unconventional attire of jeans and vest, a peaked cap, the only badge of his profession, pushed incongruously to the back of his head.

George slapped him on the shoulder, and the young man moved away towards the helicopter, standing squarely on the green turf. Then George turned back to Charlotte, and his words were for her alone.

"Do not look so angry," he said. "We all make mistakes."

"Alex did not ask me to go to New York with him," she told him tautly, but George's expression did not alter.

"Do wives need invitations?" he queried dryly. "I must go. *Herete, kyria. Kali thiasketbasi!*"

He strode away to climb into the helicopter, and Charlotte watched it take off with a frustrated sense of impotency. When she turned back to the villa, only Maria was waiting on the patio.

"Kyrios Alexandros?" she asked at once. "He is well?"

Charlotte's sigh was defeated. "Yes, Maria, he's well. But he won't be coming – back, for some time."

"Oh, *kyria!*"

Maria's sympathy was almost Charlotte's undoing. It would have been so easy to give in to the tears which burned at the backs of her eyes, to allow the old woman to comfort her, secure in the knowledge that Maria would believe her distress was solely to do with the news George Constandis had brought.

But she couldn't do it. She couldn't cheat the old servant like that, even though she resented George's attitude. But the tears she was tempted to shed had much more complicated origins, much of which she didn't entirely understand herself.

So she accepted Maria's condolences dry-eyed, and as soon as possible made her escape to her room to try and prepare herself for the second ordeal of the day.

Eleni Faulkner's home was little more than a cottage, nestling in a fold of the cliffs overlooking a rock-strewn cove. There was a garden surrounding the cottage, bright with flowers and shrubs, some of which like roses and hollyhocks Charlotte recognized, and others she did not. The building itself was made of stone and painted white, dazzling in the noonday sun.

Charlotte had quite enjoyed the journey across the island. Sitting in the donkey cart, she could see so much more than when she was on foot, and she had determinedly put all disquieting thoughts out of her mind.

Yanni, the old man who drove the donkey cart, spoke little English, and for this she was grateful. It meant that he, at least, was not continually asking her about Alex and his affairs. Yanni spent most of his time chivvying the donkey, who seemed inclined to stop and eat grass unless he was prevented.

The light breeze lifted the hem of Charlotte's skirt, blowing it above her knees, and she smoothed it down quickly. She had thought a long time about what she would wear for this visit to Alex's grandmother's house, and had eventually decided that this cream silk chiffon dress, with its long wide sleeves and vee neckline, was most suitable. She had put up her hair, too; for coolness, she told herself, although in truth she found a childish satisfaction in doing something of which Alex would not approve. Still, he could not disapprove of her visit to his grandmother, and the care she had taken over her appearance proved she was not quite as undaunted as she would like to believe.

Eleni Faulkner awaited her in a cool lounge-parlour. Charlotte was shown in by an elderly woman servant who regarded her mistress's guest with obvious curiosity. And why not? thought Charlotte wryly. She was supposed to be Eleni's granddaughter-in-law.

As before, Alex's grandmother was wearing black, this time with a white apron over her ample skirts. She stood in the small, over-furnished room with all the dignity of a queen receiving her subject. A dark figure against the white walls, surrounded by an assortment of furniture and bric-a-brac that would not have disgraced an antique shop. There were upright chairs and small tables, stools and cabinets, and against one wall an enormous carved dresser, set with some exquisite pieces of bone china.

"So you came," Eleni greeted her disconcertingly. "Why didn't you let me know that Alex had left the island?"

Charlotte moved uncomfortably. "I suppose – I didn't think." She paused. "He didn't let you know?"

"As I understand it, he left in rather a hurry. How could he let me know?"

Charlotte shrugged, trying not to be intimidated. "I'm sorry."

"Well, never mind. Sit down, sit down. We'll have an aperitif before lunch. Do you like *ouzo*?"

"I don't think I've tried it," admitted Charlotte, perching rather precariously on the edge of a wooden seated chair.

"What? Not tried *ouzo*?" Eleni sounded shocked. "Bettina, *feremas to ouzo, parakalo.*"

Ouzo was, Charlotte discovered, completely colourless until water was added when it became cloudy, like diluted milk. Nevertheless, she quite enjoyed its flavour, and as it seemed innocuous enough, she accepted a second.

"Now," Eleni eyed her thoughtfully over the rim of her glass, "and how are you finding life without Alex's company? Lonely?"

"I – I manage." Charlotte sipped at her drink. "As a matter of fact, I had news of him this morning."

"From Constandis, I know."

"You know?"

"Of course. He came here before coming to see you. He had a letter for me – from Alexandros."

"I see."

Charlotte digested this information without pleasure. So Alex had seen fit to write to his grandmother, but not to her. It was surprising how irritated this made her feel.

"He didn't write to you, I suppose," went on Eleni, with her usual perception. "He wouldn't. Alex was never a good correspondent – he prefers to use the telephone. But there were things he needed to say to me which could not be conveyed by word of mouth. Constandis is a good man, but he is not a member of the family, after all."

Charlotte took another sip of the *ouzo*. "It really doesn't matter," she assured the older woman tightly. "We had nothing to say to one another." And then, realising how peculiar that must sound, she added: "What I mean is – anything we have to say to one another can wait until he gets back."

"Which will not be for some time if his letter is to be believed," put in Eleni sharply.

"No. Well, that can't be helped."

"Can it not?" Eleni sounded sceptical. "Were I a more suspicious person, I might wonder if my grandson was not staying away deliberately."

Until that moment, such an idea had never even entered Charlotte's head. But when it did, there seemed such logic behind it that she actually found herself considering the truth of it. Was it possible? Could it be? Once he had had time to reconsider – to evaluate – the events of that hour before his departure, had he decided that the end did not justify the means after all?

With hot colour darkening her cheeks, Charlotte faced the old matriarch. Whatever suspicions Eleni might be nurturing, without confirmation they could mean little. "I don't think you need to concern yourself about us," she stated firmly, holding up her head. "George Constandis told me that no one else could handle this merger now that – Steiner? Is that right? – now that Steiner has been taken ill. The last thing Alex needs right now is a – a jealous wife!"

"Bravo!" Eleni clapped her hands together admiringly. "Bravely said, Charlotte. Put the old woman in her place. Tell me to mind my own business. I couldn't have said it better myself."

Charlotte's colour deepened. "That was not my intention, *kyria* –"

"Nonsense! Of course it was. Don't go and spoil it now by apologising." She paused. "Come, we'll have lunch. And I would like for you to call me *yaya*, as Alex does. *Kyria* is much too formal."

Much to Charlotte's surprise and relief, Eleni did not ask any more awkward questions. Charlotte had expected her to want to know how she and Alex met, how long they had known one another, the kind of things parents and grandparents like to know. But perhaps Alex had invented some story especially for her, and that had been sufficient. In any event, the rest of the visit passed off harmlessly, and in fact Charlotte quite enjoyed herself. Once away from personal topics, Eleni was a fascinating *raconteuse*, and as she had travelled to most of the major countries of the world, she had a fund of interesting stories with which to entertain her young guest. Charlotte was sorry when Bettina came to announce that Yanni was waiting to take her back to the villa.

"You will come again?" Eleni insisted, as Charlotte climbed up on to the cart. "Won't you?"

Charlotte smiled. "Without an invitation," she agreed. "And – thank you."

Eleni shook her head, and with a gesture of farewell walked back into the villa.

CHAPTER SEVEN

Charlotte lay drowsily on the lounger, gazing up at the arc of blue sky through the trailing leaves of the vine which had entwined itself round the pillars on the patio. She felt sleepy and lethargic, and it was only a couple of hours since she got up. She had been feeling this way for over a week, and as the temperature was much cooler now than it had been on her arrival, it could not be that which was upsetting her.

Yawning, she glanced at her watch, and as she did so she noticed with satisfaction how attractive was the light tan she had acquired. Several weeks of walking across the island to see Alex's grandmother, bathing in the sea which was still warmer than the English Channel in summer, and her earlier basking in the sun had burnished her hair and skin alike, and the added advantage of good wholesome food had covered her bones with a layer of much needed flesh. She knew she had never looked or felt so good in her life.

But these weeks of lazy self-contemplation were beginning to arouse certain anxieties inside her. It was more than six weeks since Alex's departure, and apart from that one visit from George Constandis, she had had no word to say how he was or when he would be coming back. She had told herself a hundred times that she didn't care, that she didn't want him to come back, but deep down she knew she was only delaying the inevitable. Sooner or later, he would come, or the reasons for her being here would never be fulfilled, and until they were . . .

All the same, there were times when she recalled what his grandmother had said, about his not wanting to come back. Those were difficult words to contemplate. She did not altogether understand why they should trouble her so, except perhaps that as time was a great healer, it had cast a concealing veil over the most terrifying aspects of that fateful morning. It could not really be so bad, she had told herself angrily, or people would not go on reproducing themselves with such enthusiasm. Even so, she shuddered when she remembered what he had done.

Footsteps on the patio caused her to turn her head and she saw Tina approaching with a jug of hot coffee. Lately, Charlotte had taken an aversion to coffee, but the milky chocolate smelled delicious.

Smiling, she swung her legs to the ground and sat up, only to grasp the back of the lounger sharply as her head swam dizzily. For a moment the bile of sickness surged into her throat, and she turned quite pale.

"*Kyria!*" Tina set down the jug on the nearby table, and came to bend towards her. "*Kyria*, are you feeling unwell?"

Charlotte felt the dizziness recede, and managed to look up into Tina's concerned face. "I – I'm all right, Tina," she answered, wiping the back of her hand across her damp forehead. "I don't know what it was. I just felt dizzy for a moment. I expect it's the sun. I've been out here rather a long time. I think I'll have the chocolate in the *saloni*."

"*Poli kala, kyria.*" Tina continued to regard her anxiously. "Can I help you?"

"Heavens, no." Charlotte got rather nervously to her feet but found with relief that she felt perfectly all right now. "I can manage."

It was beautifully cool in the *saloni*, and Charlotte sank down rather thankfully on to the couch. Tina set the chocolate on a table beside her, and then said: "You are sure you do not wish me to bring Maria, *kyria*?"

"Quite sure." Charlotte shook her head. "Honestly, I'm fine." She forced a smile. "I'm probably putting on too much weight with all this good food you're feeding me."

Tina shook her head. "*Ohi, kyria,*" she denied vehemently, but with a sigh she left her.

After she had gone, however, Charlotte was unable to dismiss what had occurred so easily. An uneasy suspicion was stirring inside her. Was it possible that there was something causing this lethargy, this sudden aversion for things she had previously enjoyed? And now this dizziness? She was not a fool, but she was an inexperienced girl coping with a situation she could scarcely believe. Her hand probed the smooth skin of her abdomen bare above the low waistband of her hipster jeans. She couldn't feel anything, but then what did she expect after only six weeks?

She shivered where before she had been too hot. Could she actually be pregnant? Could such a momentous event have occurred after such a disastrous beginning? Her knees shook. She felt frightened, purely and simply frightened, and there was no one she could turn to to explain her fears.

It was her own fault, of course, that she had not realized it sooner. But she had never been so regular in her habits that the events of the past couple of months could not have held up her bodily functions. Or so she had imagined. And she had not been knowledgeable enough to disbelieve what one would-be confidante at school had told her, which was that fertilization only occurred if the girl was getting as much pleasure out of the act as the man. It was scarcely credible that a living organism could result from Alex's brutal possession of her, and certainly there had been no pleasure in it for her.

Fleetingly, she thought of Eleni, but then rejected the idea. Much as she had come to like and respect the old woman, she was still Alex's grandmother, and this was something she could not bear to discuss with her. It was something so personal – so intimate – she was loath to discuss it with anyone. And yet she would have to.

Hardly aware of her actions, she poured herself a cup of chocolate and sipped the satisfying liquid slowly. What did one do on Lydros if one was ill? If one wanted to see a doctor? She couldn't believe there was a doctor on the island, and yet surely a patient would not have to make the journey to

Piraeus for medical attention.

She frowned. She would have to ask one of the girls, or Maria. Perhaps one of the girls might be best. Maria's eyes were too sharp, her perception too astute. With a little imagination, she might well guess what Charlotte was trying to hide.

After lunch, Charlotte went to take her usual rest on the bed. Unless she was going out, she invariably rested for an hour after the meal, and now she knew why lately she had fallen asleep instead of reading as she used to do.

Today, however, her mind was too active to sleep. All manner of thoughts and possibilities were spinning round in her head, and she stared up at the ceiling wondering what Alex's reactions would be. She frowned. Of course, he would be delighted. It was what he wanted, after all. The reason for her presence here made manifest. Now he would know that it was only a matter of time before he had the heir he wanted.

Charlotte found this knowledge curiously unpalatable. Her hand probed her body again and lingered sensuously. It was a tantalising thought that there could be the seed of another being growing inside her. She felt a protective sense of possession towards it, a satisfying knowledge that she was capable of motherhood.

She must have slept eventually because when she woke it was late afternoon, the shadows lengthening across the soft rugs piled on the floor. Stretching, she sat up to get off the bed and experienced the same dizzy sensation as she had felt on the patio that morning. It made her feel slightly sick, and she waited until the dizziness subsided before attempting to get off the bed. So, she thought, the evidence strengthened. She was not reassured by the thought.

When she walked on to the patio some fifteen minutes later, showered and changed into a cool lime green cotton dress, she found Eleni sitting waiting for her. She was surprised. There had been no arrangement to see one another today, and for a moment she wondered whether Eleni had had news of Alex. Her lips trembled. Surely nothing had happened?

But Eleni's expression was calm and composed as she turned from her contemplation of the flowers to greet her grandson's wife. "Ah, there are you are, Charlotte," she exclaimed, with a smile. "You sleep late these afternoons."

Charlotte could not control the slight deepening of colour which darkened her cheeks. "It's laziness, *yaya*," she told the old woman firmly. "Has Maria offered you some tea?"

"Tea? No. I don't want tea, Charlotte. I came because Maria thought to inform me that you were not well this morning."

"Oh!" Charlotte was taken aback. "Oh, I see."

Eleni looked her up and down. "I must say you look all right now."

"I am. I am." Charlotte shifted uncomfortably. "It – it was nothing. A touch of the sun, that's all. Maria worries too much. Now – will you have some tea?"

"If you insist, I suppose I must." Eleni sounded disgruntled. "You're sure you're all right?"

"I've told you, I'm fine. Don't fuss. Haven't you ever felt a little under the weather?"

Eleni relaxed. "Of course I have." She chuckled. "Very well, Charlotte. I'm sorry. But Maria's note sounded urgent. Besides ..." she spread her hands, "it was too nice an afternoon to spend alone."

Even so, after Eleni had gone, Charlotte wondered how much Maria had said in her note, and how much either of them suspected. It made the possibility of her seeing a doctor without arousing any comment that much less feasible.

The following morning, Charlotte was violently sick almost the minute she set foot out of bed. She sat there on the side of the bed, with the room revolving sickeningly about her, and wondered how on earth she could keep this to herself.

Unfortunately, Tina chose that moment to knock at the bedroom door, and although Charlotte did not have the strength to answer her, she opened the door and came into the room. It took only seconds for her to absorb what had happened, and shaking her head she insisted that Charlotte get right back between the sheets. Charlotte protested, but it did no good, and besides, she felt too ill to put up much of a struggle. She was vaguely aware that Tina went away and came back again, and presently the scent of lemon disinfectant cleared the air. She lay back against the pillows, feeling sick and frightened, and utterly alone.

"*Tora, kyria, ti simveni?*"

A cool hand was laid against Charlotte's forehead, and she opened her eyes to find Maria looking anxiously down at her. The compassion in the old servant's face was weakening, and Charlotte felt tears rolling unheeded down her pale cheeks.

Maria shook her head, smoothing the girl's hair from her forehead, looping it behind her ears. "Now – you are feeling a little better, aren't you?" she asked gently.

Charlotte swallowed convulsively. "A – a little."

"So why are you crying? You know what is happening to you is nothing to cry about, *kyria*."

Charlotte blinked. "What – what do you mean?"

Maria smiled. "Have I not delivered many babies, *pethi*? Do you think I do not know why a girl has the sickness? Kyrios Alexandros will be so pleased. And Kyria Eleni! I will send for her – "

"No!" Charlotte forced herself up on her elbows, grasping Maria's gnarled hand. "No, please – don't tell her, Maria. I – I'll tell her myself, but – but not yet."

"Ah, I understand, *kyria*. You wish for Kyrios Alexandros to be the first to know about his son. And why not? That is as it should be. I will speak to Sophia, and she will go to the village and tell Vittorio. He can go to the mainland and send a message – "

"*No!*" Charlotte sank back weakly against the pillows. "I mean – well, there's no need. Alex – Alex will come back as soon as he can. I – I don't want to trouble him."

"Trouble him, *kyria*?" Maria looked astounded. "He will not consider this a *trouble*! For many years now, Kyria Eleni has been wanting him to get married – wanting a great-grandchild. They will both be – enchanted."

"Well, I'm not enchanted," muttered Charlotte, turning her face into the pillow.

Maria chuckled. "You will be, *pethi*. We all have to suffer a little unpleasantness to begin with."

"A little unpleasantness!" echoed Charlotte indignantly. "Why? Why should we? Why should a man get away without suffering anything?"

"That is the way of the world," Maria assured her calmly. "Now, you rest a while. You'll see, in an hour you will feel fine again."

And it was true. Although Charlotte was very chary about getting out of bed the second time, the giddiness had left her and only a hollow emptiness in her stomach gave her any discomfort. This was soon banished by a cup of tea accompanied by a roll, fresh from the oven, and then she did indeed feel perfectly fit. It was amazing, and the realization lifted her spirits. Even her fears seemed exaggerated in retrospect.

Even so, for the next few mornings, she was very reluctant about getting up. She found she felt much better if she ate something before actually getting out of bed. This was Maria's suggestion, and she soon realized that a dry biscuit could work wonders on her constitution. By the end of a week she had grown accustomed to taking these simple precautions, and she could feel her body beginning to adjust itself to its new condition.

What disturbed her most now was Alex's prolonged absence. With every day that passed she became more convinced that what Eleni had said was true. He was staying away deliberately – but why? What possible reason could he have? And why didn't she send word to him as Maria wanted her to do? The old servant adopted a definite air of disapproval every time she saw Charlotte these days, but she could not appreciate the difficulties of Charlotte's position.

Then, late one evening, after Charlotte had gone to bed, she heard the sound of a boat's engines. Any sound carried easily on the still night air, and she rolled on to her stomach. lifting her head to listen more intently. Thoughts of bandits or terrorists flicked through her head, to be discarded instantly. She was not the only one with ears to hear, and the village was much nearer the channel between the headlands. All the same, it was unnerving, lying there in the darkness, wondering who it could be. She gave a thought to Alex, but he always used the helicopter, and besides, she would have had word if he was coming, she felt sure.

The engines were cut and silence descended again. Charlotte sighed frustratedly. Whoever it was, surely they could not expect her to be up at this time of night. It was almost midnight. Of course, it might be George Constandis come to inform her when Alex was due back. Her stomach muscles tightened, reminding her of what she had to tell him when he did come. Strangely, she did not want to tell him.

She rolled on to her back again, kicking over the covers impatiently. It was quite a warm night, and her brushed nylon nightgown was sufficient covering. She stared into the darkness with troubled eyes. If it was George Constandis would someone come and tell her? Or would he be expected to wait until morning? She shifted restlessly. Curiosity made her want to get out of bed there and then and go and see for herself.

There had been no further sounds and she sighed again. Perhaps she had been mistaken in thinking the sounds came from below the villa. Perhaps the wind which blew quite strongly after dark had carried sounds from the village.

She almost jumped out of her skin therefore when the bedroom door opened almost silently and a tall broad figure entered the room. He closed the door and leaned back against it, and at once Charlotte knew who it was.

"A-Alex?" she got out chokingly, and with a sigh he

crossed the room and switched on the bedside lamp.

Her first impressions of him were that he was drunk. He swayed a little as he stood there looking down at her, but there was no smell of alcohol on his breath. Then she realized he was exhausted. His eyes were red-rimmed, his face was thinner than she remembered, and lines of strain were etched between his nose and his mouth. He had unloosened his tie and unbuttoned the neck of his shirt, his dark suit creased after the long flight.

"Did I wake you?" he asked flatly, running a hand round the back of his neck. "I'm sorry."

Charlotte sat up, reaching for her silk robe. "Why didn't you let me know you were coming?" she exclaimed, more concerned for him than she would have thought possible. "Is George with you? Did you come in the launch?"

"I came in *a* launch, yes." Alex flexed his shoulder muscles tiredly. "And no, George isn't with me. I came alone."

"*Alone?*"

"Yes, alone," he returned heavily. "Are you all right?" His eyes grew cynical as she pulled the folds of the robe about her. "Don't worry, I'm not about to demand my conjugal rights. I'm too tired."

Charlotte stared at him worriedly. "You'd better sit down before you fall down," she retorted. "Can I get you anything? Some coffee? Or a sandwich?"

Alex shook his head, sinking wearily down on to the side of the bed. "No, nothing, thanks. I had a meal on the plane a few hours ago." He rested his head in his hands. "I just need some sleep, that's all."

Charlotte stared at his bent head. Now was no time to ask questions or to answer them. She didn't know why he had chosen to come back alone, or why he had come to her room instead of his own. Unless perhaps he had only intended checking that she was still there.

His breathing deepened as she watched him, and bending over him she saw to her dismay that he had fallen asleep.

Asleep – and here! On her bed!

Shaking her head, she regarded him frustratedly for another few minutes, and then, as he showed no signs of stirring, she slid his jacket off his shoulders and eased him back against the pillows. He groaned and relaxed against their softness, turning to burrow his head into them without even opening his eyes. Charlotte stood, undecided, his jacket still in her hands, and then, with a gesture of impatience, she dropped it over a chair.

His shoes came next, and she pushed them under the bed, considering his pants with doubtful eyes. Should she, or shouldn't she? If she didn't, he would be far too hot and uncomfortable. And besides, he wore under-pants, didn't he? They could be no more revealing than wet shorts.

Ignoring any doubts that still lingered, she unbuckled his belt and eased his pants down over his hips. They came off without too much difficulty, and joined the jacket over the chair. Then she sat down on the other side of the bed and wondered what to do. If she went and slept in his bedroom it would be all over the villa in the morning that she had left Alex on his first night home.

And besides, what could happen? Alex was weak, exhausted. She could be up and dressed before he opened his eyes in the morning.

With another faint sigh, she shed the silk robe, turned out the lamp, and climbed into the bed beside him. He didn't stir, and it was wide enough to permit at least a couple of feet between them. Charlotte turned on to her side and closed her eyes.

She awakened to the unusual weight of an arm outstretched across her breasts, and the warmth of another body beside hers in the bed. Immediately she remembered the events of the night before, and her head jerked sideways on the pillow, seeking to see whether Alex was already awake. But he was not. Some time during the night he had shrugged out of the shirt he had been wearing, and it now lay in the heap at the foot of the bed. A growth of beard darkened his jawline, but relaxed in sleep, the lines she had noticed the night before had been smoothed away.

Lying there, with the weight of his arm across her, the hair-roughened skin of his chest brushing her arm, and the heated scent of his body close beside her, Charlotte felt a curious sense of security. It was all she could do to prevent herself from raising her hand and touching his face. She had not realized how ridiculously relieved she would feel to see him, or how easy it would be to forget all the brutal things he had done to her.

Despising her weakness, she moved her legs from under his, but the activity disturbed him. His eyes opened and looked into hers, and the unguarded desire in their depths caused her to tremble. She knew she had to move, to get away from him, but she seemed mesmerized by his gaze. Almost in slow motion, she felt the arm across her breasts move, his hand sliding caressingly over her shoulder to her nape. Slowly, but insistently, he drew her quivering body closer, and with unhurried deliberation began to kiss the creamy skin of her shoulders. He pushed the offending straps of her nightgown aside, and trailed his mouth across her throat to the hollow between her breasts.

"Alex . . ." she got out chokingly, "Alex, please . . ." but he paid no heed to her protests. He was intent on arousing her to a full awareness of her own physical needs and a strange lethargy that deprived her of the strength to get away from him was weakening her limbs. She actually found herself moving against him, feeling the quickening of his desire, her hands seeking the hardness of flesh and muscle that was crushing her beneath him. Then her mouth encountered the parted urgency of his and resistance ceased.

"Dear God, Charlotte," he groaned, burying his face in her hair, "why did I stay away so long?"

Charlotte did not answer him. She was no longer responsible for her actions, winding her arms around his neck, grasping handfuls of his hair and dragging his mouth back to hers. She wanted him to go on, and if she considered what she was inviting, she did not care. At least, not then. Her body demanded satisfaction, and her mental processes were temporarily submerged by Alex's demands upon her. When he took possession of her, she prepared to suffer in silence, and then was overwhelmed by forces she had not known existed inside her. She was engulfed in pleasure, transported into a golden world which Alex seemed to share. With a muffled little cry, she wound herself closer against him, uncaring at that moment for anything but him...

CHAPTER EIGHT

CHARLOTTE stirred reluctantly. Someone had just knocked at the bedroom door, and the harsh sound brought her back to the cold world of reality. She was hastily pulling up the covers when Tina came into the room carrying the usual tray of tea and biscuits. The girl stopped abruptly when she saw her master sleeping soundly beside her mistress, and for once Charlotte saw she was disconcerted.

"*Pardon, kyria,*" she exclaimed, in a whisper. "I – I did not know Kyrios Alexandros was back!"

Extricating herself from Alex with difficulty, Charlotte moved to the side of the bed, breathing a sigh of relief when he did not waken. "Just put the tray here, Tina," she said softly, indicating the bedside table. "You can tell Maria that your employer arrived back unexpectedly late last night."

"*Ne, kyria.*" Tina nodded vigorously, and set down the tray, her eyes lingering somewhat enviously on Alex's sleeping form. Then her eyes shifted to Charlotte, desperately holding the thin sheet in front of her. "*Ne, kyria,*" she said again, and with a little smile she left them.

After she had gone, Charlotte chewed on a biscuit. Surprisingly this morning she had not felt particularly nauseated, but as her brain began to function again she rested troubled eyes on her husband.

So that was what the lecturers at school had meant when they had warned the girls of the traitorous aspects of their own bodies. She could recall every detail of what had occurred with uneasy clarity, conscious of the shameless way she had abandoned herself to him. She had actually wanted him to make love to her, although she doubted that that tender emotion had played any part in Alex's behaviour. He was a man, and he had *wanted* her. But love didn't enter into it.

That was what made her part in it so – so degrading somehow.

And it had all been for nothing, after all. She should have stopped him. She should have told him that there was no need for him to touch her ever again. She was already pregnant. She had conceived the child he had gone to such lengths to obtain, and there was no longer any necessity for him to pretend.

But instead, what had she done? Her cheeks burned with remembered humiliation. She had allowed him to hypnotize her, to use that undoubted expertise he possessed to arouse a response inside her which, once kindled, had scorched her in the blaze of its intensity. Oh, she had been a fool all right, a stupid fool! Because she now knew that he had the power to seduce her whenever he chose. And when he discovered that she was already pregnant, who knew what construction he might place upon her actions? How could she bear the ignominy of confessing such a thing to him? And if she didn't tell him, Maria would!

Stifling a groan of self-disgust, she slid out of bed, running involuntary hands over her own nudity. Then, aware that he might wake at any time, she quickly pulled the folds of her robe about her. She was not a moment too soon, Alex was stirring, and with an exclamation she fled into the bathroom.

When she returned to the bedroom, she found to her surprise that Alex had gone. Contrarily, she didn't know whether to be glad or sorry, and when she realized that Maria might see him at any time and blurt out her congratulations, she hastened into her clothes with undue speed.

The button on her jeans was tight, and she wrinkled her nose in surprise. Then her breathing quickened. Of course, already her waistline was thickening. In a month's time, she would be unable to keep her secret from anyone.

Taking a deep breath, she fastened the button, and then rummaged in a drawer until she came up with a loose-fitting cotton smock with a scalloped edge. It was an attractive garment, and she thought with relief that these days smocks were not wholly confined to pregnant women.

Leaving her room, she walked quickly along to the hall, and encountered Maria changing the flowers in a bronze vase. The old woman straightened excitedly when she saw Charlotte, and said: "Tina tells me that Kyrios Alexandros is home! You must be very happy. What does he say about . . ." She flicked her hand knowingly towards Charlotte's stomach.

Charlotte glanced apprehensively behind her, but they were alone and not being overheard. "Maria, he doesn't know," she stated quietly.

"Not know?" Maria threw up her hands. "You have not told him?"

"I – no. No, I haven't."

"*Then sas katalaveno, kyria.*" Maria sighed, shaking her head. "I do not understand. Why have you not told him?"

Charlotte shifted restlessly from one foot to the other. "Nine months is a long time, Maria. Anything could happen – "

"And probably will if you do not tell him, *kyria*," retorted Maria sharply.

"What do you mean?"

"Ah, *kyria*, have I not known Alexandros since he was a small child? He is very much a man, no? He has been away many weeks." She shrugged helplessly. "You understand what I am trying to say, *kyria*?"

Charlotte was scarlet. "Yes. Yes, I think so. But you don't have to worry about that. Nine months – "

"Only a little over six months in my estimation, *kyria*," Maria interrupted her. "I am not blind. I have eyes to see. But understand this, you have been here some time now, and I have grown fond of you . . ."

"I'm very pleased to hear it." Alex's drawling masculine tones startled both women, as he came down the shallow steps into the hall. "Now, Maria," he went on, putting an affectionate arm about her shoulders, "what has Charlotte been doing to make you look so worried?"

Maria glanced significantly at Charlotte and the girl held her breath. But after a moment, the old woman answered: "She – she isn't eating enough." She paused. "I think she misses you, *kyrie*."

Alex glanced at his wife, but Charlotte refused to meet his eyes, and he looked away again. "Well, I'm back now, Maria." He hesitated. "And *I'm* ravenous! Where are those warm rolls I've been tantalising myself with the thought of ever since I went away?"

Maria excused herself and went to attend to his breakfast, but not before she had cast a rather reproving look in Charlotte's direction which Alex intercepted. Charlotte, however, only waited for the old woman to disappear before turning and walking along the corridor towards the patio. She wanted to put some distance between herself and her husband. But he followed her.

She walked jerkily across the tiled area at the back of the villa, where she had spent so many hours while he was away. As she scuffed her toes, a quick look over her shoulder assured her that he had stopped by the open doors, supporting his shoulder against the jamb. In close-fitting denim jeans that moulded the muscles of his thighs, and a sleeveless denim waistcoat which left most of his chest bare, he was disturbingly attractive, the more so because she knew what had put that lazy indolence in his walk. Last night he had been tired and tense, someone she could feel compassion for. This morning, after the sensual satisfaction of their lovemaking, reasserting his male dominance, she told herself she hated him.

And yet she could feel her skin prickling just to contemplate the touch of his hands upon her. His hands and lips had explored every inch of her body, and the pagan delight he had inspired in her made her yearn for him to do it again. But he must never know that – this man who had taken her as payment for a wager, whose only intention was to plant his seed inside her. How easily he had succeeded, she thought bitterly, aware that in some despicable way she was wishing it had taken some considerable time . . .

Now Alex flexed his shoulders muscles lazily. "You're brown," he said, surveying her with his head tilted to one side. "It suits you."

Charlotte did not answer, and he went on: "What have you been doing with yourself while I 've been away? Have you been bored?"

Charlotte shook her head. No, bored she had not been. Restless, maybe, towards the end of the time he was away. But she had her own reasons for that.

Alex's expression hardened slightly. "What's wrong? Have you stopped speaking to me or something?"

Charlotte took a deep breath and turned. "No," she said shortly. "Of course not."

Alex's brows drew together. "Charlotte, don't let us have to start all over again. We both know things have gone too far for that."

"Was that why you stayed away?" she flared hotly.

He sighed. "No. Well – perhaps partly." He straightened, moving away from the door towards her. Looking down at his bare feet, he went on: "I could say that the merger took longer than we expected. It did. I only got through there two weeks ago. But – well, I couldn't come right back."

Charlotte stiffened. "Why? Is there someone else?"

"No!" His retort was angry. "No, there's no one else. My God, Charlotte, you have some opinion of me, don't you?"

She flushed. "I only meant – "

"I know what you *only* meant. Anyway, no. There's no one else, as I say. But – oh, God! you know as well as I do how you were when I left. Dear heaven," he raked a hand through his hair, "you certainly know how to make a man feel a dog!"

"You hurt me!" she defended herself, in a small voice, and he nodded resignedly.

"I know, I know. But there was no way... Do you think it didn't hurt me, too?" He halted before her, and she looked up at him with wide curious eyes. "You have a lot to learn about me, Charlotte. I'm not an automaton, you know."

"Aren't you?" Charlotte held up her head. "What are you trying to say?"

"I'm trying to say, I had – doubts."

Charlotte's courage wavered. "About – coming back?"

"Yes."

She licked her lips. "Wh-why?"

"You ask me that?" His voice was harsh, and he pressed his balled fist against his thigh. "Charlotte, you may not believe this, but I felt sorry for you, sorry for the things I'd done. Even if your father didn't deserve any better, maybe you did – "

"Anyone can make a mistake!" Charlotte burst out feelingly. "If Daddy really was a compulsive gambler – "

"Oh, he was, believe me!" Alex's lips twisted sardonically.

" – well, if he was, you must have driven him to the end of his tether!"

"Charlotte! For God's sake, this wasn't the first time – " He broke off, turning violently away. "God, how did we get on to this topic? I wanted to talk to *you*!"

Charlotte felt a quiver of apprehension feather along her veins. "No, wait. What do you mean? This – wasn't – the – first – time?"

"Forget it!" Alex took a deep breath, and at that moment Tina appeared behind him.

"*Parakalo*, Kyrios Alexandros. *To proyevma*," she ventured shyly, simpering under his gaze. Without a backward glance, Alex went towards her.

"It's good to see you again, Tina," he responded in English, smiling down at the Greek girl. "Come on! Show me those rolls before I die of starvation."

Giggling, Tina led the way into the villa, and left to herself, Charlotte turned away and walked towards the lounger

Maria always set out for her. But she was too restless to sit down. She felt upset and frustrated, not altogether sure what Alex had been trying to tell her. One thing did seem certain. His visit to her room the night before had not been intended to pick up where he left off before he went away. When he had fallen asleep, she should have woken him up and sent him back to his own room. Then this morning's – incident – would not have occurred.

But what good would that have done? she argued with herself. It was already too late to have doubts, although Alex was not aware of it. She frowned. It was possible, she supposed, to have an abortion. It was not yet too late. But ... She pressed protective hands over her abdomen. No! Whatever happened, she could not permit that. Not when there was no reason why she should not produce a perfectly healthy baby. This thing, this foetus which was growing inside her, was already a living being, and she could not contemplate taking its life for any reason.

But what should she do? Sooner or later, Alex would have to know about the baby. Perhaps though she should wait and discover exactly what his intentions might be. Tugging the darkening leaves from a hanging clump of bougainvillea, she stared unseeingly towards the lemon grove, unaware of the island's beauty beneath the cooling autumn skies. What had Alex meant about her father? Why couldn't he tell her the truth? He must know that whatever her father had done had been only weakness, not criminal irresponsibility.

Eventually she sought the relaxation of the lounger, stretching her length comfortably. She expected Alex to come looking for her when he had finished his breakfast, and she intended to continue their conversation. But he did not return, and she lay there resentfully, feeling the cool breeze bringing goose pimples to her arms. With an exclamation, she got up and went into the villa, refusing to admit that she was curious about Alex's whereabouts.

Tina was clearing the table, humming happily to herself,

but Charlotte regarded her dourly. "Where is my husband?" she demanded, ignoring the dictates of reason, and Tina pointed towards the closed library door.

"*Eki, kyria,*" she answered politely, but Charlotte suspected she had her own reasons for the small smile which accompanied this information.

Descending the steps into the hall again, Charlotte approached the library door rather tentatively. She wondered why Alex should choose to spend his first day at home indoors, and whether she ought to mind her own business.

But it was her business, she argued impatiently. He knew she would be waiting for him to come and finish their conversation. Was he deliberately being awkward?

Collecting all her courage, she flung open the library door. Alex was seated at the square oak table which occupied a central position, a briefcase open beside him, its contents strewn across the table's surface. He was obviously working, and he looked up rather impatiently at her entrance.

Charlotte halted uncertainly in the doorway, and then deciding she could not retreat gracefully after that entrance said: "What are you doing?"

Alex pushed back his chair and rose to his feet. "What does it look as if I'm doing?"

Charlotte rubbed her nose with her finger. "Working, I suppose."

"Right first time!" Alex was sarcastic. "What do you want? Is something wrong?"

Charlotte's breathing quickened. "Is it too much to expect a little of your company on your first day home?"

Alex stared at her mockingly. "*You* want *my* company? That was not my impression earlier on."

Charlotte flushed. "Oh, what's the use?"

She turned and would have marched out of the room, but he covered the space between them, caught her arm and drawing her back inside the room, closed the door.

"Now," he said quietly, without mockery, "I'm working because George is due in about an hour, and I want to have these figures ready for him. I intended to do them last night, but – " he broke off, "as you know, I didn't."

"So that was why you came back!" stormed Charlotte angrily. "To get some figures!"

"Among other things," he conceded. "Charlotte, I tried to tell you – "

"And George is coming to collect these figures?"

"No." Alex hesitated. "No. He'll be staying a few days."

"Staying?"

"Yes. There's some organising to be arranged. We can work just as well here."

Charlotte gasped. "I gather from that you didn't intend to do so. What changed your mind?"

"Oh, *Charlotte*!" Her name was a remonstrance on his lips. "Charlotte, for God's sake – " He raked a hand through his hair. "Look – okay, so I didn't intend staying. I told you about that. But now I am."

"Why?" Charlotte's lips had begun to tremble so she clamped them tightly together between words. "Because you changed your mind again after this morning?" She clenched her small fists. "Well, you don't need to bother about me. You don't have to stay here, or assert yourself ever again!" She pulled up her smock to reveal the button of her jeans which she had had to unfasten. "I'm putting on weight, Alex. Can you guess why?"

Alex stared at her as though he didn't believe her, his eyes dropping the length of her body with disturbing intensity. Then he came towards her, staring down at the place which was now hidden beneath her smock again.

"You're telling me you're pregnant?" he said, in a strange, uneven tone.

"Well, if I'm not, I don't know what's wrong with me!" she retorted, coldly flippant.

Alex's expression was grim. "Don't make jokes!" he

commanded harshly. "My God, how long have you known this?"

"Two – maybe three weeks."

"Three weeks! Why wasn't I informed?"

"Oh, sorry, sir, but you weren't here, sir!"

"Stop it!" Alex's fingers suddenly bit into her upper arms. "Hell, Charlotte, I had a right to be told, didn't I?"

"Well, now you have been. No one else knows. Except Maria, and perhaps the girls."

"And my grandmother?"

"No. I made Maria keep it to herself."

"Why?"

Charlotte shook her head, her momentary surge of provocation leaving her. "I – I didn't want anyone to know," she admitted in a small voice.

"Why not?" Alex sighed heavily. Then he shook his head. "I never dreamt – I didn't think . . ." He paused. "And you? How do you feel?"

"Me?" Charlotte's lips twisted. "Oh, I'm fine – fine! I can't drink coffee, I'm sick every morning unless I eat dry biscuits before getting up, and I get tired after spending only a couple of hours on my feet! I'm really fit!"

"Charlotte!" He shook her gently. "Charlotte, please!" His eyes were troubled, and she felt a ridiculous urge to reassure him. But why should she? She hadn't asked to be made his wife, to be brought here and forced to bear his child! Everything he did had a purpose behind it, and right now all he wanted was to assure himself that *his child* was receiving proper care!

"Leave me alone!" she exclaimed, dragging herself away from him. "How do you expect me to feel? All soft and gooey, broody like a mother hen! Well, I don't. I don't – I don't want this baby!"

That this wasn't strictly true was something that Charlotte could not admit, even to herself, but Alex did not know this. With a sigh, he turned away and went back to his desk.

"You knew the terms of the contract," he told her flatly.

"Yes. Yes, I knew them," she told him angrily. "But I didn't sign anything, did I?" She turned to the door. "I'm going to see your grandmother. Don't expect me back for lunch."

"Now wait a minute." Alex came after her again. "Why are you going there? You can't go alone."

"In your absence," she stressed the words, "I've had to do everything alone. And besides, your grandmother has a right to know that she's going to be a great-grandmother, doesn't she?"

"Wait until this afternoon and I'll come with you."

"What? And have you gloating over the way you've proved your manhood? No, thanks!"

Alex put his hand against the door, blocking her departure. "I can prove my manhood with you any time I like!" he bit out savagely, and she trembled. Then his hand fell away from the door. "Oh, go on. Get out of here! But don't leave the villa!"

Charlotte made no reply, but she knew she would not obey him. His wife she might be, the unwilling mother of his child – but his slave she was not.

She saw the helicopter coming in low over the headland as she walked across the cliffs towards Eleni's cottage. The cottage lay some distance beyond the village, but it was easier circling the centre of the island than clambering over its rocky formations. Once Alex had taken her to the village and introduced her to Vittorio's wife, Nana, but since he had been away she had not liked to intrude on the lives of his employees.

By the time she reached the cottage, Charlotte was exhausted. It was over a week since she had walked here, usually finding it easier to summon Yanni and his trap. But this morning to have done so would have aroused Alex's attention, and that was the last thing she wanted.

Eleni was in the garden of the cottage, pulling up some

weeds, her hands protected by a pair of stout rubber gloves. She looked up in surprise when she saw Charlotte, and exclaimed: "Did you not see the helicopter? Perhaps Alexandros is back!"

Then she noticed Charlotte's pale face, and her expression changed. "*Pethi mou*, what is the matter? You are ill?"

Charlotte shook her head wearily. "Oh, no – no. Not ill. I — " She ran the back of her hand across her damp forehead. "I seem to be running a slight temperature, that's all."

Eleni took off her gloves and taking Charlotte's arm guided her towards the cottage. "Come in, come in. Come inside," she said, urging the girl before her into the cool dimness of her overcrowded living room. She settled Charlotte in a chair and then summoned Bettina. "*Kafes,* Bettina," she ordered the old servant peremptorily, but Charlotte moved her head slowly from side to side.

"No, not coffee," she managed weakly. "Just – tea, or water."

"Water?" Eleni turned to look at her in some surprise. Then she turned back to Bettina. "*Poli kala, tsai,* Bettina. *Ghrighora!*"

Nodding, Bettina went to do her bidding, and Eleni came to Charlotte, lifting one of her limp hands and shaking her head anxiously. "Alex will wonder where you are."

"He won't. I told him I was coming here," replied Charlotte truthfully.

"You *told* him?"

"Yes. Oh, he got back late last night. That would be George in the helicopter you saw."

Eleni allowed Charlotte's hand to resume its languid position on the arm of her chair. Then she folded her own hands and regarded her grandson's wife intently. "If Alex just got back last night, what are you doing here today?" She frowned. "You have been – arguing, *ohi*?"

Arguing? Charlotte felt a little sick. "You might say that," she agreed tiredly.

Eleni made an irritated sound with her tongue against her

teeth. "Why? Why have you been arguing? I'm sure Alex would be delighted to hear he was to become a father, wasn't he? Or haven't you told him that?"

Charlotte's eyes flicked open. "You – know? What has Maria been telling you?"

"Maria has told me nothing. Good heavens, I did not need to be told. I guessed a week ago when Maria sent for me, that's all. You were almost convincing, but I have had babies of my own, Charlotte. And although I may be old, I am not blind."

Charlotte straightened her back, sitting upright in the chair. "Well, at least it saves me having to tell you," she said flatly.

Eleni uttered an impatient ejaculation. "What is the matter, Charlotte? Have you told Alex? If not, you must."

"I've told him," Charlotte retorted shortly, and looked up as Bettina carried the tray of tea into the room.

Tea on Lydros was not the same beverage as Charlotte was used to drinking in England. It was made from camomile and other herbs, and while it was hot and fragrant, it was infinitely different. Nevertheless, she had grown accustomed to it, and right now it was very welcome. There were biscuits, too, still warm from the oven, and after two of these, Charlotte's feeling of nausea had left her. She remembered she had had little breakfast that morning, but Alex's presence had stifled her appetite.

Eleni presided over the cups, seated beside the small table where Bettina had placed the tray. She was only a few feet away from Charlotte, and the girl could sense her silent disapproval.

"What is it?" Charlotte asked at last, feeling more able to cope now that she was no longer feeling empty inside. "I thought you liked me coming here. I hoped you'd ask me to stay to lunch."

Eleni looked at her impatiently. "My dear child, you know how much I enjoy your visits. And as to lunch, what I have is yours. But – " She paused, absently pleating the folds of her apron. "You have to understand, Charlotte, Alex is my grandson. I love him dearly. And you are his wife. If you are unhappy, he must be unhappy, and that I do not like."

Charlotte heaved a sigh. "I didn't say I was unhappy."

"No. But it is obvious, isn't it? You would not be here otherwise."

"*Yaya*, Alex has brought work to do. George is here because there is work to do. He – that is, Alex said that George is staying, for several days. My presence at the villa is – is just a nuisance."

"Ah, I see." Eleni looked a little less strained now. "You are angry because Alex brings work to do when your time together has been so limited so far."

Charlotte opened her mouth to protest, and then closed it again. Why not let Eleni think that? What harm could it do, after all? At least it would stop her from worrying. She would see only what she wanted to see, and anyway, the facts seemed to bear it out. Only Charlotte knew the truth. And Alex himself, of course.

"Can I stay to lunch, then?" she asked, and Eleni nodded her grey head.

"Why not? Why not? If I know Alex, it will not be long before he comes looking for you." Her smile reappeared. "You may not realize this yet, *pethi*, but Alex can be a very jealous man!"

If she had thought to reassure Charlotte by these words, she was wildly off key. To consider Alex's reactions when he found her gone made Charlotte's nerves tingle. To imagine him coming here, looking for her, almost made that craven part of her change her mind about staying.

CHAPTER NINE

CHARLOTTE and Eleni were drinking tea after lunch when Sophia arrived. The girl was hot and breathless, her cheeks flushed from hurrying in the heat of the day. Bettina brought her into the parlour, and Eleni regarded her frowningly.

"*Kala, ti thelete?* What is it?"

Sophia glanced resentfully towards Charlotte resting comfortably on the couch, and Charlotte guessed what she was about to say before she opened her mouth.

"Kyrios Alexandros sent me to find his wife, Kyria Eleni," she replied stiffly. "We have been worried about her. Kyrios Alexandros has had us all searching the villa."

Eleni turned questioning eyes in Charlotte's direction. "I thought you told me that Alexandro knew where you were?"

"I did." Charlotte put down her tea cup and swung her legs resignedly to the floor.

"Wait!" Eleni gestured for her to stay where she was. "What are you doing?"

Charlotte sighed. "I thought you expected me to go with Sophia."

Eleni shook her head vehemently. "Do not be so foolish. You cannot leave immediately after the meal. Besides ..." She turned to look again at Sophia, "why did not Kyrios Alexandro come himself?"

"He is working, *kyria*. Kyrios Constandis is here. They have been working all morning."

"Then Alexandro cannot expect his wife to wait around for him to find the time to speak with her," Eleni retorted sharply. "You may tell your master that his wife is in safe hands. I will see that she gets home safely, *ohi*?"

"*Ne, kyria.*" Sophia subjected Charlotte to another of those hostile stares. "*Efharisto.*"

Eleni instructed Bettina to give Sophia a drink before she left, but after she was gone Charlotte shifted restlessly on the couch. "Why does she dislike me so much?" she exclaimed, half to herself, but Eleni had heard her.

"Sophia's mother used to work at the villa when Sophia was a little girl," she explained. "Alexandro was already a young man, of course, but he took time out to play with her when she accompanied her mother. He was fond of her, as he is of all children. But Sophia did not see it that way. She adored him, she still adores him. She is jealous of you, that is all. And why not? You are younger than she is. Perhaps when she realizes you are to have Alexandro's child, she will accept you."

Charlotte found that very doubtful. Besides, after the child was born, she would be going away. Who would Alex get to take care of the baby? She found the thought that it might be Sophia something she did not care to contemplate.

Conversation lapsed, and Charlotte saw that Eleni's head was nodding. She felt drowsy, too, but she could not relax. Soon she would have to return to the villa and face Alex's annoyance that she should have dared to disobey him.

Bettina was serving tea at four-thirty, and Eleni was just asking her to arrange for Yanni to take Charlotte home when the powerful roar of the helicopter's engines rent the quiet afternoon air. Charlotte's mouth went dry at the sound. Surely Alex wasn't leaving again without even saying good-bye? Couldn't he at least have waited until she got back? Devastatingly, she knew that she didn't want him to go.

She caught Eleni's eyes upon her, but she could give the old woman no reassurance. She sensed that Eleni was as anxious as she was herself, and her lips parted helplessly.

But the noise was increasing, not fading away, and with an exclamation Charlotte scrambled off the couch and rushed to the windows. The helicopter was landing, on the cliffs a few yards from the cottage, and she could see that Alex was alone behind the controls.

She turned and looked at Eleni. "It – it's Alex," she said, unnecessarily.

Eleni's hands relaxed their hold on the arms of her chair. "Well, you'd better bring another cup, Bettina," she said, with enviable calmness. "It seems we have another visitor."

Alex strode into the cottage unannounced, his eyes going straight to Charlotte, still standing beside the windows. Then he went towards his grandmother, taking her hand and bending to kiss her cheek. As he did so, Charlotte watched him. He had changed out of the jeans he had been wearing earlier, and was now more formally dressed in a bronze silk suit and matching shirt. His attire disturbed her anew. On the island he did not wear suits, silk or otherwise.

"So, Alexandro," Eleni was saying now, "how are you? It is so long since you went away."

Alex straightened, his eyes flickering coldly over Charlotte, releasing himself from his grandmother's clinging fingers. "I am sorry," he apologized without enthusiasm. "The situation was more complicated than I had imagined."

"But you are back now, and that is the main thing," remarked Eleni with satisfaction, unaware that Alex was looking at Charlotte again, silently stripping her of any defence she might raise against his obvious anger.

Then Alex turned back to his grandmother. "I may not be staying long," he stated bleakly.

Eleni looked up at him then, her eyes wide and troubled. "Not staying?" She turned to Charlotte. "What is this?"

Charlotte moved her shoulders uncomfortably. "I don't know."

"Don't you?" Alex seemed intent on humiliating her. "Of course you do. Why don't you tell my grandmother the truth? That you didn't want me here? That our marriage was a mistake, and that you'd prefer to be free!"

Charlotte gulped. "I – that's not true!" Her cheeks were

scarlet as she gazed imploringly at Eleni. "I don't know why he's saying such things," she exclaimed. "Just because I left the villa when he asked me not to . . ."

Alex's eyes bored into hers. "And the rest," he said harshly.

"Alexandro! Alexandro, please!" Eleni rose to her feet to face them. "You're behaving like children, not responsible adults! Good heavens, it's natural that after being separated for so long you should both have problems of readjustment. Charlotte has become used to doing as she likes. You cannot come home and make demands on her without giving reasons!"

"Charlotte is expecting a baby!" muttered Alex roughly. "She should not be walking here!"

"I know that. And she knows that. She was exhausted when she arrived. But is that any reason for you to – how do the Americans put it? – blow your chimney?"

"Your *stack*!" put in Alex drily. He raked a hand through his hair. "You don't understand, Grandmother."

"Don't I? Well, perhaps not. But as Charlotte is in – her condition, you should not be shouting at her simply because she shows a little independence."

"Independence!" muttered Alex irritably. "I asked her not to come here. I specifically asked her to stay near the villa."

"I'm not a child!" exclaimed Charlotte tremulously.

"I suggest we all sit down and have some tea," said Eleni quietly. "Then, afterwards, you can take Charlotte home, Alexandro. In that monstrous machine, if you must."

"There was nothing else to hand," remarked Alex briefly, and Eleni conceded this with a dismissing gesture.

Tea was served, but Charlotte did not enjoy it, and she did not think Alex enjoyed it either. But he was tolerably polite to his grandmother, answering her questions about the merger, telling her that New York had been cold and wet, that it was good to be back in the sunshine again. Then Eleni brought up the subject of Christmas, and Charlotte realized, with a sense of disbelief, that it was only a couple of weeks away.

"Franco is coming, of course," Eleni was saying thoughtfully. Then, to Charlotte: "Franco is my brother. He is a widower, and lives in a village not far from Athens. But he always joins us for Christmas, does he not, Alexandro?"

Alex nodded, seeking permission to light a cheroot. Charlotte had noticed that he did not smoke often, but when he did it was almost always cheroots.

"Consider," said Eleni musingly, "next year Christmas will begin to mean something again. There will be a baby in our family once more."

Charlotte got up and walked away. She could not bear to think of where she might be twelve months from now.

The journey back to the villa was accomplished in silence. It was a short hop, and George was waiting for them when they landed. He slid open Charlotte's door and helped her out of the helicopter, commenting on how well she was now looking.

Charlotte forced a smile. "It's good to see you again, Mr. Constandis," she said, and he shook his head.

"George," he insisted, walking with her towards the villa.

Charlotte went straight to her bedroom, and was not surprised when Alex came after her. He closed the door and then folded his arms, staring expectantly at her. "Well?" he said at last, when she did not speak but picked up a brush and began to tug the bristles through her hair. "So you are not so brave, after all."

Charlotte took a deep breath. "I don't know what you mean."

"Why didn't you tell my grandmother why I married you? Why didn't you complain to her how I forced you into this, how I exacted *complete* payment for your father's debts?"

Charlotte sank down on to the side of the bed. "Why should I do that? Why should I humiliate myself in such a way?"

"You would have humiliated me more!"

"Would I?" Charlotte hunched her shoulders. "Well, I – I wouldn't hurt your grandmother like that. I like her too much."

"But you'd like a miscarriage more!"

"*No!*" Charlotte's eyes were wide and pained. "No. No, I wouldn't, damn you!"

Alex's eyes narrowed. "You said you didn't want the baby."

Charlotte bent her head. "I don't. But I wouldn't – do anything to hurt it."

"So why did you tramp two miles across the cliffs?"

Charlotte sighed. "I've done it before. Lots of times."

"She said you were exhausted," he reminded her harshly.

"I – I was. All right, maybe, it was foolish. But you – you made me do it."

"*I* did?" He came towards her then, sitting down on the bed beside her. "How am I to blame?"

Charlotte swallowed convulsively. This near, he was too disturbing. She was very much afraid that if he touched her she would break down completely, and that was the last thing she must do. But she could remember only too well what had happened between them on this bed a few short hours ago. And she sensed he was not unaware of it himself. But to him, it had been a physical experience, the necessary accompaniment to his desire for a child. While to her ...

She moved, putting some space between them, and said: "You – you can't expect me to behave like – like one of your employees!"

"Do I expect that?" he enquired, his lips thinning.

"Yes. You think you can *tell* me what to do, and when I don't conform, you're furious!" she retorted.

"I'm sorry. I was merely thinking of what was best for you."

"For the baby, you mean."

"All right, if that's the way you want to see it."

Charlotte hunched her shoulders. "I don't need your concern."

"So what do you need?"

"Nothing – nothing."

"Are you sure?" He caught her shoulders and swung her round to face him. "That was not my impression this morning."

Charlotte's lips parted in dismay. "That's a rotten thing to say!" she choked.

"But apt, don't you think? I mean, I didn't know about your condition. But you did!"

Charlotte managed to find the strength to pull herself away from him. "All right," she agreed unsteadily, "I can't deny that. Enjoy the feeling of mastery it gives you. But – but just remember, any man with sufficient expertise could arouse an inexperienced girl!"

Alex got stiffly off the bed, his expression grim. "I see. So now we know where we stand, do we not? When I need – relief, I come to you. And when you feel the same ..."

"Oh, don't go on!" Charlotte pressed her hands over her ears. "You can be so cruel, can't you? God, I wish I'd never married you!"

"Do you think there aren't times when I don't feel exactly the same?" he demanded savagely, and left her.

While George was staying at the villa, Charlotte saw little of her husband, except at mealtimes. Both men spent at least part of the day closeted in the library, and part out on the boats. Once they both flew out in the helicopter, and Charlotte thought they had gone for good. Then late in the evening they flew back again, and life resumed its pattern. But never once did Alex come to her bedroom, and there were times when, in spite of herself, she wished he would. She told herself it was natural that she should feel she needed him sometimes. This was his child she was carrying inside her.

Why shouldn't he bear some of the anxieties she was suffering alone?

Christmas, and all the things it had meant in England, seemed a million miles away from this remote island, and although there were few people she wanted to send cards to, she wished she had the opportunity to do some shopping, if only to try and feel the spirit of the season.

She mentioned the matter to Eleni one afternoon when the older woman was visiting the villa, and she advised her to speak to Alex. "Athens may not be London," Eleni told her frankly, "but there are some excellent stores, and I'm sure you would be able to buy everything you wanted there."

Charlotte felt sure she could, too, but mentioning the matter to Alex was something else again. Nevertheless, she felt she had to make the effort, if only to assure herself that she dared to do so, and over dinner that evening she brought the subject up.

"You want to go to Athens?" Alex considered her words unsmilingly. "Do you think you should?" His meaning was obvious.

"I'm not an invalid," Charlotte replied shortly, aware of George Constandis's eyes upon her. "Actually, I've never felt better now that I don't feel sick in the mornings."

Alex crumbled a roll on his plate. "Very well. When would you like to go?"

"As soon as possible."

Alex frowned. "Is tomorrow soon enough?"

"Tomorrow?" Charlotte's eyes widened. "Tomorrow would be – marvellous!"

"Good." Alex lifted his soup spoon. "We'll take a break tomorrow, George. You don't mind flying my wife to Athens, do you?"

"George!" Charlotte had uttered the man's name almost involuntarily. "I mean, won't you be taking me, Alex?"

"I don't think that's necessary," replied Alex, spooning

soup into his mouth. "I have work I can do here while George is away."

"Oh, but – " Charlotte's disappointment was out of all proportion to the request denied. She pressed her lips tightly together and stared down unseeingly at her dish. She was dangerously near to tears and she despised herself for her weakness.

"Surely you can take the day off and fly Charlotte to Athens, Alex," George was saying now. "I'm sure she'd prefer your company to mine."

"Do you think so?"

Alex's words were sardonic, and Charlotte wondered how much of their curious relationship he had relayed to his assistant, and what George really thought of their marriage.

"Please." Charlotte lifted her head proudly. "I don't mind, Mr. Constandis, honestly. I'm just sorry you've been given the chore."

"It is no chore, and my name is George," he answered firmly. "Very well. What time would you like to leave?"

Charlotte shrugged. "Would ten o'clock be suitable?"

"Eminently," replied the older man smilingly. "I shall look forward to it."

But Charlotte did not. She was doubtful as to the effects of flying in her condition, and if she had to be ill, she would have preferred it to be Alex with her. But then she chided herself. George was more likely to be sympathetic than her husband, and no doubt he had more patience.

Still, she did not sleep very well that night with the unexpected outing ahead of her. It was so long since she had been in contact with other people, and she was ridiculously nervous of leaving the island. She awakened soon after seven, and was bathed and dressed by the time Tina arrived with her tray of morning tea and biscuits.

She had decided to wear a dress for a change, a simple pinafore style dress with a high waistline fitting just beneath her breasts which successfully hid her condition from all but the most discerning eyes. The dress was cream, splashed with orange, which amazingly did not clash with the copper gold brilliance of her hair, and wedge-heeled shoes did marvellous things for her morale. Studying her reflection in the wardrobe mirrors, she was satisfied she had never looked better, and it was with a sense of impatience she had to concede that pregnancy suited her.

Alex was seated at the dining table when she came along the corridor, lean and masculine in a blue denim shirt and close-fitting denim pants. A matching jacket was slung carelessly over the back of his chair. He was stirring his coffee with an air of abstraction, but he rose at her approach and his eyes narrowed beneath his heavy lids.

"Well," he drawled sardonically, "is this all for George's benefit?"

Ignoring his sarcasm, Charlotte seated herself at the table and rang the bell for Tina. After ordering rolls and more tea, she felt more capable of dealing with her husband. He had reseated himself, and although he appeared to have finished his meal, seemed quite content to sit and watch her every movement with the unnerving intentness of a cat with a mouse.

"Er – where is Mr. Constandis?" Charlotte asked, unable to sustain his stare for long.

"George, believe it or not, is indisposed," replied Alex dryly.

"Indisposed?"

"Unwell – sick – ill; to put it in plain language, incapable of flying the helicopter."

"Oh!" Charlotte was not as disappointed as she might have been. "I – I'm sorry. Is it anything serious?"

"You want my opinion? I don't think there's anything wrong with him."

"Nothing wrong with him ..." Charlotte halted. "I don't understand."

"Oh, I should have thought it was pretty obvious. *Obviously*,

George thinks that if he is indisposed, I'll have to take you to the mainland myself."

Charlotte pushed back her chair. "Well, you can disabuse him of that idea right away, can't you," she retorted tautly, turning to leave him. But Alex got up also, and his fingers curved round her upper arm as she would have passed him.

He looked down at his brown fingers against her creamy flesh, moving his thumb in a caressing exploratory motion. "Don't walk out on me, Charlotte," he advised her quietly. "You're looking very beautiful this morning, and right now I can think of things I'd rather do for you than flying the helicopter, do you understand me?"

Charlotte's breathing quickened. "Let me go," she said, and heard the annoying tremor in her voice.

"Providing you'll sit down again and eat your breakfast," he agreed, his eyes frankly sensual as they rested on her mouth. "And I shall be taking you to Athens, whether you like it or not."

Charlotte looked helplessly up at him. "I wanted you to take me," she protested. "But you refused!"

"Yes. Well, now I've changed my mind. Right?"

She nodded mutely, and to her relief he let her go. He held her chair while she reseated herself, and then when Tina arrived with her tea and rolls he excused himself.

Charlotte's appetite had not been stimulated by the knowledge that he had only to touch her to reduce her to a trembling mass of nerves and sensations. Nevertheless, she knew it would be foolish to get on board the helicopter with an empty stomach, so she put all disruptive thoughts aside and silently thanked that small being inside her which demanded sustenance whatever her mental condition.

Alex came back as she was finishing, and slid his arms into the sleeves of the denim jacket. "It's raining," he said, regarding her critically. "Still want to go?"

Charlotte nodded. "Can we?"

"Of course. If you're ready. Bring a mackintosh."

"I – I have to pay a call first," she told him in some embarrassment, but Alex was not perturbed.

"I'll see you here in five minutes," he said easily, and she nodded with relief.

Charlotte had expected Vittorio or Dimitrios to accompany them, but when she joined Alex by the helicopter, he was alone. He was wearing a black leather jacket over his denim suit, and drops of water glinted on his thick straight hair. He helped Charlotte inside without a word, and then walked round the machine to join her.

Charlotte looked at him doubtfully as he fastened her safety straps and showed her how to use the headset. "Isn't Dimitrios joining us?" she asked.

Alex straightened to adjust his own gear. "No. Did you expect him to?"

Charlotte sighed. "Alex, you know what I mean. Shouldn't there be someone – that is – " She broke off. "Don't take risks because of me."

Alex put on his headphones and smiled mockingly at her. "And don't you pretend a wifely concern at this late stage," he returned wryly. "Comfortable? Fine. Here we go!"

The journey was not half so comfortable as the journey to the island. The rain was relentless, and the wind buffeted the helicopter continually. The islands below were shrouded in a mist of vapour, and few ships had ventured out on an unusually choppy sea.

Alex was unperturbed, and spoke to her often through the microphones, pointing out the larger islands and telling her a little of their history. They almost achieved the closeness and companionship they had known in that week before Alex left for New York, that week before their relationship was irrevocably changed. But while they could never again share that almost platonic friendship, in some ways their association was deeper now and more intimate than before. Charlotte was aware of this even though she endeavoured to reject it.

They landed at a private flying club some distance from the

city, and had a drink in the clubhouse while Alex phoned for a car. The chauffeur who had met them the day they landed in Athens from London arrived soon afterwards in the sleek black limousine Charlotte remembered, and he drove them into the city.

Even through the rain, Charlotte could admire the classic beauty of the Parthenon towering on the hills above the city and Alex promised that the next time he brought her to Athens he would take her up to the Acropolis. *The next time* – Charlotte found she liked those words, even if she had to acknowledge that if it was another three months before she visited the city she would be in no condition to trail around the tourist attractions.

Shopping was tiring, even using the car. Charlotte was not used to the crowds of people thronging the streets, the honk of horns and the scream of brakes, and she found it all a little overpowering. Alex was the only friendly face she saw, and after becoming separated from him once, she took his arm and held on ot it.

But it was pleasant to see the gaily decorated shops, the coloured lights and painted icons. The trappings of Christmas had a similarity the world over, and Charlotte couldn't help the wave of homesickness which suddenly filled her. Last Christmas she had spent with her father, at a ski resort in Austria. It was only now she remembered he had spent a lot of evenings at the casino.

They had lunch at a large restaurant overlooking Constitution Square. Syntagma Square, Alex told her, was the Greek name, and Charlotte thought she liked the sound of that better. They ate grilled prawns and *moussaka*, the latter a little rich for Charlotte's taste, and finished with cheese and figs. The cheese, too, was stronger than she cared for, but Alex appeared to have no such reservations. Sitting across the table from her, attractively relaxed, he obviously enjoyed the food, and the casual conversation he conducted put her completely at her ease. Some Greek musicians played throughout the meal, and the whole atmosphere was exciting.

During the afternoon, Charlotte bought some cards, and a few small presents for Cristof, Maria and the girls. Alex left her at one point to make a phone call, and while he was away she purchased a hand-woven shawl for Eleni, and a long-playing record by one of his favourite recording artists for Alex himself. She had not a lot of money to spend, and although Alex had told her he had accounts at most of the larger department stores, she could not bring herself to use his name. So far it had been an anonymous day, the two of them mingling with the crowds like any other shoppers. She did not want to draw attention to his identity, anyone might hear, and even if it was ridiculous, she genuinely cared what happened to him. Besides, she did not want to buy *his* present with *his* money.

A plastic carrier advertising a favourite brand of vermouth successfully concealed her purchases from Alex's discerning eyes, and when he suggested they ought to be leaving, she was only too willing to agree. It had been a long tiring day, and she looked forward to getting home again. *Home?* What an impressionable idiot she must be, she thought angrily. Already she was thinking of Lydros as home, when in a few months her presence there would no longer be required.

She was quiet on the journey back to the island, answering Alex in monosyllables when he spoke to her. Truthfully, the painful thoughts she had had earlier were not wholly responsible. The taste of aubergines was strong in her throat, and she wished she had not eaten the cheese. She tormented herself with the question of what she would do if she actually needed to be sick, and in the confined space of the cabin it was a terrifying possibility.

Alex became aware of her discomfort towards the end of the journey. To begin with all his energies had been taken up with controlling the helicopter, and he had had no time to query her apparent hostility. But when he took a proper look at her pale face, he shook his head impatiently.

"Why didn't you tell me?" he demanded. "You feel sick, don't you? God, what am I? An unfeeling monster, that you shouldn't dare to tell me?"

Charlotte sighed. "What could you have done?"

"I could have put the helicopter down on one of the other islands. It has been known in an emergency, you know."

Charlotte looked apologetic. "Actually, I feel a bit better now. It – it was the *moussaka*, I think. And perhaps the cheese."

"You're sure you're all right now?" he insisted.

Charlotte nodded. "We'll be landing soon, won't we?"

"Yes. Yes, we will." Alex turned his attention back to the controls. "But in future, remember that I have a vested interest in your wellbeing."

Charlotte thought she hated him at that moment. She didn't care that he might have been hurt at her determination not to share her anxieties with him, or that he might genuinely worry about her. To her, that cold statement summed up his reasons for anything he ever did for her.

CHAPTER TEN

ELENI's brother arrived two days before Christmas, but he was not alone. He had brought his granddaughter with him.

Irena Kalamos was a beautiful Greek girl, perhaps a year or two older than Charlotte, with lustrous dark hair and eyes edged with sooty black lashes. Like many Greek women, she did not favour the fashionable slenderness so popular in the west, and her curves were roundly voluptuous. Her clothes fitted closely, emphasising the fullness of her breasts, the provocative swing of her hips, and her eyes rested on Alex with evident approval.

Charlotte met the visitors on the day of their arrival. Dimitrios had flown to the mainland to bring Franco Kalamos to Eleni's cottage, and it had been arranged that the two older people should join Charlotte, Alex and George for dinner that evening.

However, when Alex was told that as well as his great-uncle, a distant cousin had also arrived, he decided that Eleni could not possibly accommodate them both at her small cottage. In consequence, Franco and Irena arrived at the villa late in the afternoon, full of gratitude for Alex's thoughtfulness.

Meeting Irena for the first time, Charlotte wished Alex had consulted her before offering them their hospitality. Although she knew she had no reason to feel that way, she disliked the other girls's immediately monopoly of her husband's conversation, and an emotion she refused to identify curled her hands into fists every time she heard Irena's provoking laugh.

She was dressing for dinner that evening when Alex came into her bedroom. He was already changed, his dark attraction accentuated by the maroon silk shirt he was wearing together with black suede pants that clung to the powerful muscles of his legs. Charlotte, wearing only a thin slip, was supremely conscious of her own vulnerability, and she felt his eyes resting on the slight swell of her abdomen. Then his gaze shifted to her face, his lips twisting at her startled expression.

"Please," he said, "don't be alarmed. I have not come here to seduce you. But ..." he glanced round, "I have given Franco my room and I wondered if you have any particular objections if I slept in the dressing room adjoining this."

Charlotte expelled her breath on a gasp. For a minute she had thought he was about to suggest sharing her room, and the mixed emotions this had aroused frightened her. Far from objecting, she might well have welcomed his suggestion, but it was fortunate she had not had to make that choice.

"I – well, no," she managed jerkily. "Providing – "

"I shan't intrude on you more than I have to," he retorted sharply. "I may need to use the bathroom, of course, but that's all."

Charlotte shrugged awkwardly. "It's your house."

Alex regarded her coldly. "Yes, it is. Thank you for your indulgence." And he left her.

Charlotte wore a long yellow caftan that evening, its plainness relieved by dark brown frogging all the way down the front and wide sleeves decorated with the same brown braid. Its fullness only hinted at the slender curves beneath, but the low neckline in front drew attention to the tantalising hollow between her breasts.

Irena, in rich red satin, could not have provided more of a contrast, her skirt moulding her body like a second skin. Scarlet fingernails lingered against Alex's sleeve as she drew his attention to what she was saying, and Charlotte resigned herself to remaining in the background.

Eleni had joined them for dinner, and Charlotte was not surprised to hear Alex suggesting that she should come and stay at the villa, too, while her brother was here. Eleni said she would think about it, but obviously she found the idea appealing. She and Franco saw one another so rarely, and would naturally have plenty to talk about.

Charlotte found herself with George Constandis when they went to have dinner, and was pleasurably surprised when Alex insisted that she took the seat beside his. Of course, Irena occupied the seat at his other hand, and during the course of the meal Charlotte found herself turning more and more to Alex's assistant for conversation. Irena did her best to monopolize Alex's attention, and Charlotte could feel a burning resentment smouldering inside her. She refused to identify it as jealousy, but that was what it was, and she felt she would like to scratch Irena's eyes out.

When the meal was over, coffee was served in the lounge, and Charlotte was ensconced on the couch beside Franco Kalamos. He was an elderly man, tall like his sister, but without her stature. He stooped a little, and his hair was very thin, but he had a charming smile which he used to good effect. Tina brought in the tray of coffee and set it beside Charlotte, and when she said she did not take any herself, he said:

"Do you not like our strong beverage, *pethi mou*?"

Charlotte managed to control her colour. "I used to like it," she murmured unobtrusively.

"I see." The old man's eyes grew thoughtful. "And do you not find life on Lydros rather isolated after London?" he added. "London was where you had your home, was it not?"

"That's right. I suppose Lydros is isolated, as you say. But I like it."

"Eleni has been telling me that Alexandro has been away a lot since your marriage. That is most unfortunate."

Charlotte forced a smile, conscious of Irena laughing at something Alex had said as they stood together by the recording deck. "I – we manage," she replied politely, and Franco nodded.

"Alex works very hard. We had all given up hope of his ever getting married. So many of our young women have tried to trap him, but to no avail." His eyes twinkled. "You see the effect he has upon poor Irena. She is quite enchanted by him, do you not think?"

Charlotte glanced their way, her eyes unknowingly hostile. At no time could she imagine herself feeling sorry for Irena. She was far too confident and sure of herself.

Franco seemed concerned that what he had said might have been taken the wrong way, and went on: "I am sure you had no difficulty in that line, *pethi*. It is obvious from the way Alex looks at you that you have a very special place in his thoughts."

Charlotte felt a tight constriction in her throat. It was kind of the old man to try and reassure her, but she knew very well that Alex had no such gentle feelings towards her.

George came walking across to join them. "It was a delicious dinner, Charlotte. Did you choose the menu?"

Charlotte coloured then. "No. That is – Maria deals with that. I'm afraid I know very little about Greek cookery."

"But you should learn," exclaimed Eleni, overhearing their conversation. "It was different in the beginning. Nobody expected you to come and take over. But Maria must be made to understand that you are now mistress here."

"Give her time," remarked a familiar voice from just behind the couch where Charlotte was sitting, and she glanced round indignantly to find Alex standing looking down at her. "You have to remember, Charlotte is still very young. And our way of life takes some getting used to."

"Yes, she is. Very young, isn't she?" Irena appeared behind Alex, and the tone of her voice implied that Charlotte was scarcely out of the cradle. "It is as well you have hidden her away, Alex. You might well be accused of raiding the schoolroom, *obi*?"

Charlotte turned round again, controlling the retort which sprang to her lips. She had taken an instinctive dislike to Irena and had chided herself for it. But now she knew her instincts had not been mistaken. Irena would cause trouble, if she could.

The Greek girl's remark had aroused some goodnatured teasing and Alex took it all in good part. It was easy for him, Charlotte thought angrily. They were his relatives, he could afford to be generous. But did he realize he was making her feel ornamental and childish, someone who contributed little to their marriage? She suspected he did, and hated him for it.

Later, Alex put on some records, and Irena suggested dancing. It was a way for her to get into Alex's arms, and as she watched them together Charlotte's flesh tingled with indignation. Irena had no qualms about pressing herself close against her partner, and Alex seemed to have no objections. He danced, as he did everything else, with a lithe, easy grace that communicated the power of latent energy, and while she abhorred Irena's presence, Charlotte found herself watching her husband almost hypnotically. Once he intercepted her gaze over Irena's shoulder, and his lids narrowed to shadow his eyes. But then the Greek girl said something and his brooding expression dissolved into amusement. He did not ask Charlotte to dance, and nobody seemed to expect it. She was left to talk to George and Franco, with Eleni inserting a comment here and there.

Around eleven, Charlotte decided to go to bed. Eleni had been persuaded to stay the night, and although the party looked like going on for some time yet, Charlotte had had enough. She excused herself politely, pleading a headache, and ignoring Alex's suddenly hostile expression left the room.

In the bedroom, she took off her caftan and walked wearily into the bathroom. She was tired, and she did have the beginnings of a headache, but they were mental conditions as much as physical ones.

She took a shower, luxuriating in the fall of the water against her flesh, twisting and turning beneath the flow until a tingling warmth enveloped her. Then she towelled herself dry, and tossing the shower cap aside was pulling on her silk robe as she re-entered the bedroom.

The door to the dressing room stood wide, and she frowned, running questing fingers through her tumbled hair. She could have sworn it had been closed when she first entered the bedroom. Then, before she had time to formulate any decision, Alex appeared in the open doorway, his shirt unbuttoned to the waist, his feet bare.

Immediately her breathing became ragged, and she had to control the tremor in her voice, as she asked: "What are you doing?"

Alex flexed his shoulder muscles. "What does it look like I'm doing? I'm going to bed, of course. What else would I be doing when my wife chooses to retire?"

"I – but – there was no need – "

"I choose to think there was."

Charlotte held up her head. "Why? Has Irena gone to bed too?"

Alex's mouth tightened. "Not so far as I am aware."

"I'm surprised," muttered Charlotte, turning her back on him, and picking up her hair brush. "Perhaps you should go and find out!"

"What's it to you?" he snapped.

"I – why, nothing. Of course."

"So why make that kind of bitchy remark?"

Charlotte shook her head. "I am – *supposed* to be your wife."

"So?"

Charlotte half turned towards him, her eyes sparkling angrily. "Well, what kind of relationship do you suppose your uncle will think we have if you spend your time pawing his niece?" she demanded.

"I was not – *pawing* his niece!" retorted Alex coldly.

"All right. Letting her paw you, then!"

Alex came right into the room, halting a short distance from her, obviously controlling his temper with difficulty. "Irena was not pawing me!"

"Oh, no?" Charlotte couldn't prevent the challenge. "Then what would you call it? Or is it some old Greek custom

I don't know about that permits an unmarried girl to flaunt herself in front of any married man who takes her fancy?"

"*Charlotte!*"

"Well! I mean it. The way you were dancing, it – it was disgusting!"

Alex covered the space between them, grasping her by the shoulders. "Believe it or not, but Irena does not attract me in *that* way at all!"

Charlotte stifled a gulp. "No? You must be a tremendous actor, then!"

"Oh, Charlotte!" There was an agonized torment in his tone. His hands slid over her shoulders and down her back to her hips, impelling her towards him, moulding her body to his so that she was made overwhelmingly aware of the fact that if Irena did not arouse him, she most certainly did. "Charlotte, God – don't you know? It's you I want, you I need. And if I've succeeded in making you jealous, then I'm glad. Because I don't know how the hell I'm expected to sleep in there knowing you're only a few feet away."

His hands cupped her head, turning her face up to his, and with a feeling of inevitability, Charlotte felt her mouth moving eagerly under his. What was the use of denying it? She had been jealous. And she wanted him, too. Her hands were as urgent as his as they slid his shirt off his brown, muscular shoulders, and the world slid away ...

Things looked different in the morning. She awakened with a delicious sense of lethargy which was swiftly dissipated by the discovery that she was alone in the bed. A check on her watch advised her that it was after ten o'clock, and a little of her anxiety eased. Alex was not a late sleeper at any time, and with guests in the house ... Guests!

Charlotte got out of bed, swaying a little as a trace of dizziness attacked her. She had not been troubled by it much lately, but hunger was gnawing at her stomach, and she guessed this was the reason for her lightheadedness. Alex must have told Tina not to disturb her.

Alex!

As she took her bath, she allowed the memory of the previous night to envelop her. It had been a devastating experience, a complete submergence of herself in a mutual consummation of their need for one another. Alex had been gentle and considerate, demanding and passionate, teaching her how to please him and in so doing please herself. She had welcomed the urgency of his desire, discovered that making love could last for hours and hours. Little wonder she felt so lazy this morning.

But gradually, as she lay there, a little worm of anxiety threaded the veil of indolence. What was she doing, lying here, luxuriating in a relationship which to Alex meant no more than a satisfaction of his senses? What manner of woman was she that she could find such enjoyment in reliving what had been after all just a sexual experience?

She levered herself upright in the bath, the clouds of fantasy dispersing rapidly. What was the matter with her, day-dreaming about a man who had been indirectly responsible for her father's death and who had forced her to marry him to produce an heir? Was she going mad, that she could actually betray her father's memory in this way?

She finished washing and stepped out of the water, wrapping herself in a bath towel. She was a fool! Hadn't she just granted him licence to do with her as he willed, and all for no purpose except his own self-gratification? And why? Because he could arouse her senses, because she liked his hands upon her, because she delighted in the hardness of his male body against hers?

She threw the towel away and reached for her underwear. Yes, those things were true, but there was something else, something which even now she was loath to even consider. Her feelings for Alex had changed. She still hated him at times, hated his power over her. But more important was the realization that her reasons for allowing him into her bed were not just the simple ones of mutual wanting and need. Subtly and elusively, almost without her being aware of it, he had become important to her, desperately important. He was no longer just the man of whom her father had despaired, the jailor who had taken her as his prisoner, the relentless plunderer of her innocence. He was her husband, in every sense of the word, and she was in love with him.

She found Eleni and Franco lingering over their coffee at the table, but there was no sign of anyone else. After greeting her, however, and asking after her health, Eleni enlightened her.

"Alex has taken Irena to the mainland," she told Charlotte casually, unaware of how this news might affect her grandson's wife. "You were still sleeping when they left, so Alex did not like to wake you."

Charlotte gripped the edge of the table tightly. "Why – why would he do that? Take – Irena to the mainland? She only arrived yesterday."

"Oh, I think she had forgotten some last-minute shopping," replied Eleni lightly. "Sit down, *pethi*. You look quite pale, doesn't she, Franco? It's just as well Alex didn't suggest you should go with them."

Charlotte sat down because she felt that if she didn't she might easily fall down. But her appetite had fled, and this time it refused to respond to other demands. When Eleni summoned Tina and ordered the usual tea and rolls, Charlotte felt physically sick, and it was all she could do to remain where she was. Why had Alex agreed to take Irena to the mainland? Surely he must have known how she would feel about it? Or didn't he care? Those protestations last night – had they been no more than a means to an end? A way to get her to agree to his demands when he must have suspected she was likely to refuse?

But what more could she expect in all honesty? Alex had never, at any time, professed love for her. Lust, yes – desire, of course. Never the emotion which he had so carelessly aroused in her. She had been a fool ever to think otherwise, to delude herself with thoughts that he could not have made such unselfish love to her without feeling anything more than passion. What was it he had said, about when he needed relief? That he would come to her. And he had. And she had allowed herself to be duped by it.

As soon as she could, she escaped outside. She needed to be alone, to have time to think and to plan. One thing was certain in her mind. She could not continue living like this, a brunt for his ill humour, a convenience for his sexual impulses. She had kept her part of the bargain – the *contract*. She had married him, and the child she had conceived would be born in wedlock. But there was nothing in the contract which said she had to live with him for the full nine months of her pregnancy. It didn't matter that there was no one waiting for her in England, it was still her home, and the house in Glebe Square beckoned like a shining beacon. How glad she was that she had kept the house on – her refuge, the bolthole she had foreseen herself needing. But never in such circumstances....

The isolation of the island presented the greatest problem. Had they been living anywhere where there was public transport available, she might well have written Alex a letter and left without seeing him. But Lydros's situation prevented such behaviour. She would need help to leave the island, and no one here was likely to risk thwarting their master's wishes in such a way. Besides, whatever cowardly impulses she had had in the past, she owed it to Alex to tell him what she planned to do. While she had few illusions about his concern for her, she knew he would feel concern for his unborn child, and she would have to assure him that she intended doing nothing to risk harming the baby's health.

But that interview promised to be a stormy one, and she awaited his return from the mainland with quivering anticipation. What if he tried to persuade her against leaving? she thought tremulously. What if he used the power he undoubtedly had over her to coax her to stay? How could she resist him when she loved him – when the idea of life without him looked grey and depressing?

She found a solution. So long as she remembered what he had done to her father, so long as she could summon the image of her father's bloated body after it was fished from the sea, she would stand firm.

The helicopter flew in over the villa while Charlotte was resting on the bed after lunch. She had not slept, but at least here she did not have to pretend a brightness she did not feel. Even so, she was surprised when five minutes after the helicopter landed Alex came into the bedroom. Then bitterness overwhelmed her. Of course, his grandmother would expect this kind of behaviour from him.

Nevertheless, her determination almost wavered at the tenderness of his expression, and the softness of his voice when he said: "Hello, love. How are you feeling?"

She pushed herself up on her elbows, and faced him stoically. "Do you care?"

"Oh, God!" Alex pushed his hair back off his forehead. "Of course I care."

"You do? Oh, yes, I was forgetting. If I'm not well, the baby's not well either." Charlotte was scathing. "Well, reassure yourself, we're both doing fine!"

Alex came down on the side of the bed, close beside her. In a dark green suede suit and cream silk shirt, smelling of a mixture of alcohol, tobacco and body heat, he was disturbingly attractive, and there was a moment when a small traitorous voice inside her urged her to take what he offered on whatever terms. But then sanity prevailed, and she moved her hand away from his thigh.

"What's been going on?" he asked impatiently, noticing the gesture. "Didn't Eleni tell you where I'd gone?"

"Yes. Taking Irena to the mainland. How nice for Irena! Couldn't George have done it? He was good enough for me."

Alex ground his teeth together. "You have no need to be jealous. George was with us. Or did that little item slip your notice? Irena wanted to do some shopping, and as George and I needed to go into the Athens office, she came along."

Charlotte almost faltered. George had been missing at lunchtime, but she had assumed he was working. Still, that did not alter the basic inadequacies of the situation. Alex was still using her, and would continue to do so just so long as it suited him. She didn't think she could stand much more.

Taking a deep breath, she said: "I want to go back to London, Alex."

There was several moments' stunned silence, and then Alex slowly got up from the bed. "You want to go back to London?" he echoed coldly. "Might I ask why?"

Charlotte swallowed convulsively. "There – there's nothing to stop me, is there? I mean, there's nothing in the contract about me having to live here, is there?'

Alex turned to face her, his brows drawn together in a scowl. "Let me get this straight," he said, and she realized he was shaken. "You want to go back and *live* in London?"

"Yes. Till the baby's born, anyway. Afterwards – afterwards, I might travel for a while."

"You're suggesting I should allow my wife to go and live alone in London?" Alex drew a savage breath. "Charlotte, you're out of your mind! Do you realize that if some unscrupulous villain discovers who you are, you'll be fair game for every would-be kidnapper in the business!"

Charlotte's lips trembled. "You're exaggerating!"

"Am I!" His fists balled. "Well, I won't allow it!"

"How are you going to stop me? By force?"

Alex heaved a sigh. "Charlotte, what is this? Last night – last night ... Oh, God, you know what I'm trying to say. Last night was – marvellous! Then today I'm out for what – four, maybe five hours, and when I come back you tell me you're leaving me? Charlotte, I won't let you do this to me!"

"You can't stop me!" she exlaimed, drawing up her knees

on the bed and wrapping her arms around them.

"Charlotte – "

He sat down beside her again, his hand seeking the curve of her nape under her hair. She longed to rub her neck against his hand, to allow him to draw her closer and silence her mouth with those possessive searching kisses that seemed to draw the strength out of her and left her weak and clinging to him. But she thought of her father, and flinched away.

"Don't touch me!" She almost spat the words, and he withdrew his hand and stood up again.

"So that's it!" he muttered. "You're ashamed of what happened last night. You can't reconcile the way you behaved with the way you think you ought to feel!"

"You're wrong!" she burst out, knowing he was too near the truth for comfort. "I didn't feel anything. And my flesh creeps when I think of what I let you do to me!"

Alex's face twisted. "You actually believe that?"

"I know it's the truth. All right, you can make me do things. But I don't enjoy it. And I despise myself afterwards. I hate you, Alex Faulkner. I'll never stop hating you. And I can't wait for the day when you'll have your son and I'll be free of you!"

Alex stood motionless, listening to her tirade, and when she was done, he said: "Very well. If that's the way you want it. I shan't bother you again. But I cannot and will not allow you to go and live in London!"

"What?"

He thrust his hands into his trousers pockets, unknowingly tautening the cloth across his thighs. "I am not prepared to allow you to risk your life regardless of your feelings towards me. But – " he paused, " – as my presence here appears to be the problem, I am prepared to stay away until after the child is born. Arrangements will be made for a doctor and nurse to come and stay at the villa several weeks before the baby is due, and you will receive every attention. Indeed, I have today contacted our own doctor and asked him to come and examine you next week, just to make sure everything is well. After the birth – well, as you say, that is something else."

Charlotte listened to him with an aching heart. Of course that was what she wanted, for him to stay away from her. And she could see that she would be safer here, among people who cared about her, than alone in London. But how could she deprive him of his home – even temporarily?

"You can't do that," she protested. "What would your grandmother think?"

"A lot less than she would think if you left me and went back to London," he retorted rather wearily. "Well? Does that meet with your approval?"

"This island is your home . . ."

"I have many houses – apartments." He walked towards the door. "Home is a word I rarely use." He looked back at her. "You do appreciate that I will have to stay over the next few days, until Christmas is over? I promise not to get in your hair. I'll have to sleep in the dressing room, but you can lock the door if you like."

Charlotte could feel the prick of tears behind her eyes. It was always like this. He could arouse her compassion without even trying, and she knew a moment's despair for her weakness.

Then she squared her shoulders and straightened her back. "I shan't lock the door," she said steadily. "You're my husband. You have a legal right to share my bed."

"Cold comfort," remarked Alex bitterly. "No, thanks."

The door banged behind him.

As luck, or perhaps fate, would have it, Charlotte was not at all well on Christmas Day. She had developed a severe cold from somewhere, and consequently had a ready-made excuse not to join in the family celebrations.

She was touched, however, by the presents she received in return for her small gifts; a knitted scarf from Maria, sheepskin mules from Tina and Sophia, an embroidered handkerchief from Cristof. Irena had bought her some perfume, rather an exotic blend, which Charlotte secretly thought would suit the other girl far better than herself, Eleni produced a finely stitched smock which would come in very useful later and even Franco had a box of candies for her.

All of them were going to the service at the small church in the village that morning, but before they left Alex came in to see her. She had not seen him alone since the afternoon two days ago when she had told him she wanted to leave, and as she had left his present with the others in the lounge, she had not expected his personal thanks.

"I have a small present for you," he told her, standing just inside the open door, his eyes guarded. "If you feel up to it, I'll fetch it in."

Charlotte looked puzzled. "If I feel up to it? Oh, I'm all right, really."

He inclined his head, and left the room, returning moments later with a squirming mass of amber-coloured fur. Charlotte clasped her hands together, staring at him with wide eyes, and he bent and desposited the creature on the floor. It was a spaniel puppy, plump and excited, careering round the bedroom with a complete disregard for the furniture.

"Oh, Alex!" Charlotte slid her feet out of bed, calling to to the dog, grasping its wriggling body as it tried to jump up at her. "Alex, it's beautiful!" Tears welled into her eyes. "I don't know what to say."

Alex regarded the picture they made with a rather grim intentness. Then he shook his head. "Don't say anything. By the way, she's had the usual injections, and I understand she's partially house-trained, although I wouldn't bank on it."

Charlotte looked from the dog to his face and then back to the dog again. "Is – is she mine?" she ventured unevenly, and heard his harshly drawn breath.

"Yes, she's yours," he told her bleakly. "A memento, if you like, of your stay in Lydros!" He walked out the door without a backward glance.

CHAPTER ELEVEN

BOTH January and February were wet months, and the winds which swept the island from the north-west kept the temperature well below normal for the time of year. The rain did not fall as it did in England, for days on end, but came in torrential downpours which could soak one in seconds. Roofs streamed, waterbutts overflowed, and paths were turned to muddy quagmires. The island looked different beneath its pall of water, but Charlotte had come to like it in all its guises.

She walked every day, exercising the spaniel bitch which she had named Suki. Suki demanded a lot of attention in those early weeks, and Charlotte was glad of her company. She had never trained a dog before, but it was a challenge, and in no time Suki was properly house-trained, and less likely to tug on the lead when she went walking. Her undemanding affection was a salve to Charlotte's bruised emotions, her antics a constant source of amusement. Even Maria was not immune to the appeal of those wide brown eyes, and the animal became a favourite with all the servants.

Charlotte spent most of her time in or around the villa. Since Alex's departure, she had seen little of Eleni, and she knew the old woman blamed her for what she saw as the breakdown of their marriage. On the rare occasions Charlotte had made the trek across the island, she had been made aware of Eleni's disapproval, and in consequence their relationship lapsed. Charlotte was sorry about this. She genuinely cared for the old woman. But perhaps she was right. There was no point in getting involved when in six months or so she would be leaving the island for good.

To help pass the time, Charlotte began spending part of each day in the kitchen, encouraging Cristof to teach her the preparation and cooking of Greek dishes. At first, he was not enthusiastic, but gradually, as he became interested in his subject, the lessons became a regular thing. Charlotte learned how to prepare an egg and chicken soup, which Cristof told her was a national dish, she made *moussaka*, and her own favourites, *loukmades*, which were little balls of dough, fried, and served with cinnamon and castor sugar, and melted in the mouth. She also learned a little more of the language, and providing Cristof spoke slowly enough, she could almost understand what he was saying.

The worst times came at night, when she wandered restlessly about the corridors of the villa, dreading the moment when she would have to go to bed. Doctor Leonides, the Faulkner family physician, now made regular visits to the island to check on her health, and he had given her some tablets to help her sleep. But something inside her rejected that artificial sedation. Instead she read, often until the early hours, and finally fell asleep from exhaustion, her book sometimes still in her hands. Maria disapproved of this practice, but there was nothing she could do about it.

Even so, generally, Charlotte's health was good. She ate, because she had to, she got plenty of exercise,and although she was putting on weight, it was all in the right places. Charlotte thought it was a curiously unreal time, her stomach swelling out of all proportion, and an innate disbelief inside her that she could actually be having a baby. Then the baby moved and after that Charlotte didn't question any more.

There were times when she felt an intolerable longing to see Alex. No matter how she tried to erase it, his image was constantly in her thoughts. It was not unnatural in the circumstances. Living here in his house, on his island. How could she be expected to forget? she asked herself bitterly. Sleeping in the bed where he had taught her the secrets of her own deep emotional nature. But, she suspected, no matter where she went she would feel the same. Particularly after the baby began to stretch and awaken to an awareness of its own strength.

Towards the end of March, when the winds were subsiding and the island was beginning to blossom with all the flowers of spring, she had a visitor. From time to time, Vittorio or Dimitrios had visited the villa bringing news of Alex's whereabouts and checking that all was well, but when the helicopter appeared on the horizon, Charlotte could feel her nerves stretching to screaming pitch.

But she was sitting on the patio, apparently quite calm, when it landed, and she hid her shattering disappointment when George Constandis climbed out of the cabin.

She was unaware of the change in her until George commented upon it. Three months had put a bloom on her skin, a shine on her hair, and a generous coating of flesh over her bones. The finely stitched smock she was wearing over a pair of old denim jeans barely concealed the swelling roundness of her stomach, but George thought she had never looked lovelier.

When Tina had served them with chocolate, and she had assured him that she was well, she said urgently: "Why have you come, George? Is – is anything wrong?"

George's expression twisted wryly. "I could take that the wrong way, you know. Am I not welcome here?"

Charlotte sighed. "You know you are. It – it's marvellous to see another face after all these weeks. But . . ."

"I know. You're worried in case I'm here for some other reason."

Charlotte nodded. "Yes."

George looked down into his cup. "You want to know how Alex is?"

"Of course." Her response was revealingly eager.

George hesitated. "Alex – well, he is in London."

"London?"

"Yes."

"He's well?"

"He's not ill, if that's what you mean."

Charlotte frowned. "What does that mean?"

George drank some of his chocolate, aware of her impatience as she waited for him to answer her question. "It means," he said at last, "that I am not happy about him."

Charlotte moved restlessly. "Go on."

"Well, I think he's driving himself too hard. And there's no need. He employs men to do the worrying for him, and then takes over their decisions himself. He's not eating properly, I don't know when he takes his rest. And he looks – well, tired."

Charlotte got up from her chair and paced across the patio, turning back to stare at him. "Why are you telling me this?" she exclaimed frustratedly. "Why don't you tell Alex?"

"Do you think I haven't?"

"Does he know you're here?"

"Yes. He wants first-hand news of you."

"But – he didn't ask you to tell me this, did he?"

"What do you think?"

Charlotte shook her head. "He wouldn't."

"I won't argue with that."

She sighed, walking back to her chair. "So why have you told me?"

"You could ask him to come back," replied George quietly.

Charlotte flushed. "Here?"

"Where else? It's the only place where he relaxes. No phones – no communications of any sort. He needs it, Charlotte. Something's bugging him, and I guess it's you."

Charlotte twisted her hands together. Then she took a deep breath. "George, Alex doesn't care about me. I don't know what he's told you about why we got married, but – well, it wasn't for love."

"I know exactly why you got married," answered George steadily. "I also knew your father."

Charlotte quivered. "You'll understand then how I feel."

"In a way. But you don't know the whole truth, do you? Or you might understand Alex better."

Charlotte frowned. "What do you mean? The *whole* truth? Of course I know the whole truth. Or I wouldn't be here."

George raised his grey eyebrows. "I doubt it somehow. You knowing the whole truth, I mean. Alex isn't that kind of man. He wouldn't tell you. He's too – proud."

"What are you talking about?" Charlotte was getting quite agitated now. "What don't I know?"

"How well did you know your father?"

"How well did I know my father?" Charlotte frowned more deeply. "How well does any daughter know her father?"

"No, seriously. You were away at school a lot, weren't you? You couldn't possibly have known about his gambling, could you?"

Charlotte stiffened. "I don't believe my father was a – a gambler. He played cards, yes. He was unlucky. But so are lots of people. And they don't all pay with their lives!"

George shrugged. "Oh, well, if that's the way you feel."

She stared at him helplessly. "George! George, you can't introduce something like this and then just drop it. If you know something about my father that I don't know, you should tell me."

"Would you believe me?" George tilted his head to one side. "You didn't believe Alex, did you?"

Charlotte looked down at her hands. "Alex wanted someone to give him a child with the least possible effort!"

"If you believe that – if you really believe that . . ." George shook his head. "Well, I'm sorry for you, Charlotte, I really am. I'm sorry for Alex too. I should have thought you'd have learned by now what manner of man your husband is."

Charlotte blinked. "Then tell me!"

"No. It's not up to me to explain Alex's actions. He wouldn't thank me for it. But some time, I think you should contact those solicitors of yours in London, and ask them if they know what happened eight years ago."

The weeks immediately following on George's visit were

the longest Charlotte had spent. In spite of what George had said, she could not believe that Alex's state of health was in any way connected with her. If he was driving himself, it was because he chose to do so, and if he thought of her at all it was with a sense of impatience that she should have denied him the use of the island.

All the same, she did worry about him, waiting restlessly for Vittorio's next visit so that she might ask him about his employer.

With regard to George's suggestion about writing to Mr. Falstaff, her solicitor, she was less decided. How could she write and demand an explanation for such a strange statement? The only prominent event she could recall from eight years ago was her mother's death, and surely her father had had nothing to do with that. Unless.... Unless it was her mother's death which had driven him to the compulsion which had ultimately caused his death.

Certainly she would speak to Mr. Falstaff when she got back to London, but she did not feel it was something she could write about in a letter.

The weather was getting warmer, and now she could spend hours lying in the sun. Her skin was warmly tanned and it no longer resented the sun's rays with such sensitivity. She even wore a bathing suit on occasion when she hoped no one else would see her, although her reflection in the wardrobe mirror gave her little pleasure. The baby was increasingly active now, keeping her awake some nights with its kicking and pummelling. But it was increasingly real, too, and she no longer felt entirely alone.

One afternoon at the beginning of May, she decided she would have to make the effort and go and see Eleni. She had heard nothing from Alex's grandmother since George's visit when he had paid a call on the old woman. She had not heard from Vittorio either, and she wondered, with a sense of desperation, whether Eleni was in contact with her grandson.

It was several weeks since she had walked so far, but

thankfully a cool breeze fanned her cheeks and prevented her from feeling too hot. Eleni was in her garden, gathering some herbs, but she looked taken aback when she saw her grandson's wife.

"Charlotte!" she exclaimed. "You shouldn't be walking here in your condition!"

Charlotte sighed, calling Suki and attaching the spaniel to its lead to leave outside the cottage. "I'm perfectly fit, *yaya*," she answered, following Eleni into the parlour. "Besides, the exercise does me good."

Eleni made no reply, indicating that Charlotte should sit down and ordering Bettina to bring iced fruit juice. Then, when she was seated, too, she said, "I have been meaning to come and see you myself. In three weeks the doctor and nurse arrive, do they not?"

Charlotte nodded. "I suppose so." She shivered, in spite of the heat of the day. The actual birth was looming closer now, and she had no one to turn to, no one to assuage her natural fears and anxieties.

Eleni folded her hands in her lap. "Will Alex be here when his child is born?" she asked.

Charlotte moved her shoulders in a dismissing gesture. "I don't know. Will he?"

Eleni clicked her tongue against her teeth. "Surely you will want him here then!" she exlcaimed. "I can appreciate – or at least, I am trying to appreciate your dismay at finding yourself soon to become a mother. Alex told us how you felt – that you were too young, that he had been careless. But I am afraid I cannot condone your behaviour these past months."

Charlotte digested this in silence. So that was what Alex had told his relatives – that she objected to being pregnant! Well, it was as good a reason as any, she supposed.

"Have – have you heard from Alex, then?" she ventured, and Eleni regarded her without favour.

"No, I have not. There has been no word since George's

departure. I gather you have not heard anything either."

Charlotte shook her head. "I – George said Alex was working too hard. I wondered if he had said anything to you."

"I know my grandson, Charlotte. He is driving himself because he is unhappy. And you are the cause of that unhappiness! No – " This as Charlotte would have protested. "Let me finish! When he told me he was getting married at last, I was delighted. Since his parents' death, he has been alone too much. I was doubtful when I learned how young you were, but it was obvious that Alex was in love with you, otherwise why would he have waited so long?"

"Waited – so – long?" Charlotte made a confused gesture. "What do you mean?"

"Oh, I don't want to talk about it any more. It makes me too angry," muttered Eleni sharply. "Here is Bettina with our orange juice. Let us talk of less provocative matters."

Charlotte refused Eleni's offer of Yanni to take her home. The idea of jolting along in the cart did not appeal to her, and the cooler air of late afternoon was very invigorating.

As she walked, watching Suki scampering ahead of her, she thought about what Eleni had said. What had Alex's grandmother meant about him waiting so long? Unless it was that she meant before taking himself a wife. What else could she mean, after all? She had not even heard of Alex Faulkner until eight months ago.

Charlotte was exhausted when she reached the villa, and refusing Maria's offer of tea, she went straight to her bedroom. It was marvellous to kick off her sandals and lie back against the soft pillows, feeling the aching muscles of her back beginning to relax. The shadows lengthened in the room, and she closed her eyes, falling into a deep exhausted slumber.

She awakened to a darkened room, and a distinctly uncomfortable sensation in the small of her back. Reaching across the bed, she turned on the lamp, and saw it was after ten o'clock. Maria must have decided not to wake her for dinner, but the old servant would not yet be in bed, and

Charlotte longed for a cup of tea. Swinging her legs to the floor, she stood up, slipping her feet into her sandals. Her back still ached from the afternoon's exertions, but apart from that she felt very well.

When she opened the bedroom door, she saw a light was still burning in the hall, and as she walked along the corridor and down the steps, she saw the lounge lights were still burning, too. Frowning, she approached the doorway. It was not like Maria to leave lights wasting. Then she caught her breath.

Alex was sitting in the middle of one of the skin-covered couches, his elbows resting on his knees, his head buried in his hands. He was still wearing the clothes he must have arrived in, dark suit, white shirt, his tie hanging loosely.

Charlotte hovered at the doorway, undecided what to do. And then he looked up and saw her, and a strange expression crossed his dark face. The intentness of his gaze, the way his eyes appraised her, made her glad she was wearing the honey-coloured shift which Sophia had cleverly adapted for her from one of her ordinary dresses. Sophia was clever with her fingers, and since she had had to accept Charlotte's presence at the villa now that she was pregnant, she had become very useful in that way. Eleni had been right about her at least.

"Charlotte!" Alex rose abruptly to his feet, his hands falling to his sides. "You were sleeping when I arrived. I asked Maria not to wake you."

The ache in Charlotte's back seemed to be getting worse, but she manged to ignore it. "I – I didn't hear you." She shrugged. "Did you come in the helicopter?"

"No, I came with Vittorio in the launch." Alex shifted his weight from one foot to the other, and she saw that George had not been exaggerating when he said that Alex looked weary. "I'm sorry if my visit causes you any annoyance, but I felt I should come and see my grandmother. I believe she worries about me."

"She does." Charlotte glanced behind her. "Actually, I saw her this afternoon. I went over there."

Alex frowned. "On foot?"

"As a matter of fact, yes." Charlotte sighed, unable to prevent her fingers from seeking the small of her back and massaging it vigorously. "Er – have you had anything to eat? Does Maria know you're here?"

"Naturally, she knows I'm here. And I had a sandwich. I wasn't hungry. But you must be. Maria tells me you haven't had a thing since lunchtime."

"I could do with a cup of tea," Charlotte admitted, feeling a little impatient with her own weakness. "But I'll see to it."

Alex had been watching her actions closely, and now he came over to her, moving her fingers out of the small of her back and putting his own there instead. "What is it?" he asked, and his breath mingled with hers. "Are you in pain?"

Charlotte shook her head. The feel of those hard fingers through the thin material of her dress aroused tantalizing memories, and her breathing quickened of its own volition. "It aches, that's all," she admitted jerkily. "I've probably walked too far today."

Alex began to massage her spine, a rotary motion which temporarily eased the ache. She found herself moving sensuously against his fingers, absorbed in the sensations he was unknowingly arousing, and he muttered; "*Don't*, Charlotte!" in a curiously hoarse voice.

His words brought her to her senses, and her cheeks flamed in embarrassment. "Thank you," she said. "It – it's stopped aching."

Alex's fingers stopped moving, but they remained where they were, his eyes imprisoning hers by the passion in their depths. Still looking at her, she felt his hand on her stomach, tracing the swelling mound beneath her skirt, his eyes narrowing as a small limb projected a tremor beneath his exploring fingers. Hardly aware of what she was doing, Charlotte put her hands over his, holding them against her, making him as aware as she was of the child between them.

Alex's eyes dropped to her mouth, and her lips parted invitingly. With a groan, he caught her face between his hands, and put his mouth against hers, gently at first, and then with increasing passion as he felt her instinctive response.

"Dear God, Charlotte," he breathed against her lips, "don't send me away. Please, don't send me away! Let me stay!"

Charlotte's involuntary cry brought them apart, and he stared at her with tortured eyes. "What is it? Did I hurt you?"

She shook her head mutely, putting a probing hand to the lower part of her abdomen. The pain had subsided now, but it had been a definite *pain*. Licking her lips, she looked helplessly at Alex.

"I – I think – I don't know, because I don't have any experience in these matters – but I think I might be going to have the baby," she told him steadily.

"Of course you're going to have the baby – "

"No, I mean – now."

Alex's expression was ludicrous, and Charlotte almost felt like giggling. "But you can't!" he exclaimed. "I mean, it's not due for another six weeks yet!"

"I know." Charlotte moved her head up and down. "But I think I might be."

"God!" Alex flung off the jacket of his suit, running careless hands through his hair. "Where's Maria?"

He stalked out of the room and Charlotte moved to support herself against the back of the couch. Was it possible? Could the baby be coming early? Had her walk across the island been too much for her?

She chewed anxiously at her lower lip, surprised to discover that she was not at all frightened now. Her main concern was Alex – his reactions. She didn't want him to worry about her.

Alex came back with Maria bustling behind him. "Now, *kyria*," exclaimed the old servant gently, "don't you think you are imagining it?"

Charlotte shrugged. "I don't know. I had a pain a few minutes ago, and my back has been aching since I got back from Kyria Eleni's."

Maria tut-tutted impatiently. "I knew you should not have gone so far," she exclaimed.

"So why didn't you stop her?" demanded Alex irritably. He turned to Charlotte. "Oughtn't you to sit down?" he suggested, with exquisite tenderness, but she shook her head.

"I'm all right, really. I'd like a cup of tea, though."

Alex and Maria exchanged glances, and then, muttering to herself, the old servant went away. Alex stared at his wife for a long, disturbing minute, and then he shook his head.

"Why did you do it, Charlotte? Walking all that way? You must have known it was a foolish thing to do!"

Charlotte turned away from him, resenting the reasons for his concern. "You don't have to worry," she retorted hotly. "Even if the baby is coming, it will be all right. Lots of women have seven-month babies!"

"Do you think I care – " He broke off abruptly, and took her arm. "Charlotte, please, sit down. I want to talk to you."

Charlotte allowed him to seat her on the couch he had been occupying earlier, conscious of his nearness when he sat down beside her. But before he could speak, she found herself gripped in another spasm of pain. The doctor had told her that during labour she should take several short breaths to ease the pain, and this she did, gripping the edge of the couch until the spasm passed. By then Alex's face was paler than hers, and she found herself grasping his hands and saying reassuringly: "It's all right! Oh, Alex, don't worry!"

"How the hell can I do anything else?" he demanded savagely. "I should never have considered you having the baby here. I should have made sure you were in some nursing home on the mainland well in advance."

"Well, I shouldn't have been there yet," remarked Charlotte, with wry logic. "Alex, Maria has everything ready. And I'm sure she's brought as many babies into the world as this nurse you've employed."

Alex got to his feet to pace restlessly about the room. "You can't seriously think that I would allow Maria . . ."

"What else can you do?" she asked gently. "Alex, I'm not frightened, honestly. I'm young – and healthy. And you can hold my hand."

"Oh, Charlotte!" He squatted down beside her, taking her hands and raising them to his lips. "You know I'd do anything for you, don't you?" His eyes lifted to hers. "Will you let me be there – when our child is born?"

Charlotte nodded her head. "If that's what you want."

"It is," he said huskily. "If I had my way, I'd never leave you again."

Maria came in then with the tea, and Charlotte had no time to ponder that remark. Besides, she had another spasm, and Maria gave a resigned sigh.

"Should I fetch Eleni?" Alex asked, looking from his wife to the servant, and then back to his wife again, but Charlotte shook her head.

"Why worry her?" she asked, quivering a little because Alex was still holding her hand. "We can manage, can't we?"

Alex sprawled on the couch beside her, his expression vaguely self-derisory. "I hope so," he murmured ironically. "I really hope so."

Charlotte's son was born at seven o'clock the next morning. He was a healthy six and three-quarter pounds, and lost no time in letting everyone know that he had a strong pair of lungs. Alex himself was there at the delivery, and it was he who laid their son in Charlotte's arms.

Charlotte stared down at the baby, feeling an overwhelming sense of pride and achievement, touching his rosy cheeks and stroking the silky dark hair which lay close against his head.

"Why, he looks like you," she murmured, raising her eyes to Alex's face, and he grinned whimsically.

"Who did you expect?" he asked, gently teasing, coming down beside her on the bed and looking critically at his son. "Do you really think he does?" He wrinkled his nose. "Do I screw my face up like that, and don't I have any lashes?"

"That is only because the baby is a few weeks premature," Maria exclaimed, pausing in the process of tidying the bed. "You know very well he is exactly like you."

Charlotte looked up into Alex's eyes with their thick fringe of black lashes, and her lips parted to allow the tip of her tongue to appear. "You know, you looked tireder last night than you do this morning," she said wonderingly. "And you haven't had a wink of sleep."

"Nor have you," Alex reminded her softly, but she shook her head.

"I slept yesterday evening. I must have been unconsciously preparing myself for the ordeal."

"Was it? Such an ordeal, I mean?" Alex regarded her doubtfully, but she shook her head, poking her little finger into the baby's fist, and smiling as she felt his tiny fingers closing round hers.

"It wasn't an ordeal at all," she admitted with a sigh. "Oh, I feel tired now, but it was a tremendous experience. I wouldn't have missed it for the world."

"Do you mean that?" Alex continued to look at her, and she nodded her head.

"Of course." Then she looked up at him again. "You were marvellous, too. Thank you. I don't know how you could stand it."

Alex made a teasing face at her. "I must admit, there was a moment when I felt like keeling over," he admitted. "But it was worth it. And when I saw him coming . . ." He shrugged expressively. "My son! Oh, yes, it was worth it."

Charlotte sighed again, and Maria came bustling up. "It is time you were settling down for a sleep, *kyria*," she said firmly, glancing reprovingly at her master. "And you need some sleep too, I think," she added.

She bent down and lifted the baby from Charlotte's arms, and with a regretful smile, Charlotte let him go. Then, as Maria carried him across to the hastily contrived cot, made out of one of the dressing table drawers, Alex bent his head and found Charlotte's parted lips with his mouth. He caught her unawares, and almost without thinking, she lifted her hands and put them behind his neck, holding him closely.

"Charlotte!" he muttered thickly, having to raise his arms to free himself. "*Please!*"

Charlotte sank back among the pillows, momentarily content, but a trace of anxiety darkened her eyes when, after another brief look at his son, he left the room. He could afford to be generous, she thought uneasily. He had every reason to be delighted with her. At the first attempt, she had produced the son he so desperately wanted. He must know that her part of the contract had been fulfilled to his satisfaction

But what about her? She would have been inhuman if she had not felt some emotion at the feel of her baby in her arms. And how would she ever be able to leave her son's upbringing to someone else?

CHAPTER TWELVE

Eleni arrived to see her great-grandson at lunch time, just after Doctor Leonides and his nurse had arrived in the helicopter. Vittorio had been sent to the mainland in the launch during the night to fetch the doctor and his assistant, and after they were safely landed, he flew back to Athens to collect the nursery equipment waiting at a department store.

Nurse Hani was a middle-aged woman, with an air of friendly efficiency. After Doctor Leonides had examined both Charlotte and the baby and announced them in good condition, she took charge of things, organising the household with gentle but firm competence. By the time Eleni arrived, Charlotte had been bathed and changed, the bedding renewed and the room sweetly smelling of the flowers Maria had brought in from the garden.

Alex appeared, while Eleni was ensuring that Charlotte was quite recovered from her labours, bathed and changed into beige corded pants and a cream silk shirt. He had obviously slept for a while, and Charlotte was amazed at the change in him after last night Gone was the look of weary defeat, the lines of tiredness and exhaustion. He looked vibrantly alive and masculine, and his eyes went straight to Charlotte's, exchanging with her a look of mutual experience.

"You realize walking across to see me was responsible for this, don't you?" Eleni exclaimed, as Alex walked into the room. "I told her she should not have come."

Alex came to the bed, looking down at his son nestling in his mother's arms, already turning that small mouth towards Charlotte for sustenance. "You should be flattered, *yaya*," he responded almost absently, putting out a finger and stroking a small wrist. "Not every girl would walk four miles in Charlotte's condition just to visit an old woman."

Eleni made an indignant sound. "And you should have been here to ensure she didn't do such a thing!" she countered hotly. "I trust you will be staying now."

"Oh, yes," Alex nodded, his stroking finger probing his son's tiny chin. "I shall be staying now, shan't I, Charlotte?"

Charlotte didn't know how to answer him. She didn't honestly know what he was saying. Unless he meant that as she would be leaving, he would be bound to remain. At least until someone could be engaged to take care of the child. Her heart lurched sickeningly. Oh, God, she thought desperately, she didn't want to go! She wanted to stay. Whatever he had said, whatever he had done, whatever her motives for agreeing to his infamous contract, she wanted to stay. This was her home – this man was her husband. And she loved him.

"Well, Charlotte?" Eleni was challenging her now. "Will Alex be staying or won't he?"

Charlotte licked her dry lips. "I – that's up to him, I suppose. It's his decision, not mine."

Eleni tutted irritably. "It seems to me that you both have a responsibility to your son!" she stated forcefully. She got to her feet. "I'll leave you now. It's obvious you're in good hands." She touched the baby's head. "Congratulations to you both!"

Alex escorted his grandmother out to where Yanni was waiting with the donkey cart, and when he came back, Nurse Hani was with his wife. His presence was obviously unwanted, and with a regretful shrug in Charlotte's direction, he left them.

In truth, Charlotte was still very tired, and she slept for most of the day. Then, after a light supper, the nurse gave her a sedative to see her through the night. Consequently, it was morning again before Charlotte discovered that Alex had slept in the dressing room.

Nurse Hani was eager to get Charlotte interested in feeding her baby, and although Charlotte was doubtful as to the advisability of making him dependent upon her in this way, she could not deny the thrill of emotion she felt when his seeking little mouth fastened on to her breast and began to suck, greedily. It was a painful experience in no way eased when Alex came to watch her, a curiously satisfied expression on his lean dark face.

During the next few days, they had little time alone, and even on those occasions when no one else was present, Alex seemed loath to discuss personal things. Charlotte was quite willing to allow him the delay. She did not feel strong enough to face what might be to come.

Within a couple of days she was up and walking about, much to her husband's amazement. He had obviously expected her to spend at least a week in bed, and her independence evidently did not please him. Nevertheless, there was nothing he could do about it, particularly not as Nurse Hani seemed well pleased with her patient.

After a week, Doctor Leonides asked to be flown back to the mainland. He had other patients requiring his attention, and it was obvious that Charlotte and her baby were progressing satisfactorily. Nurse Hani stayed on. She had been employed for a month, and Charlotte was glad of her assistance. There seemed so much to do, and although Maria had taken charge of the extra laundry, she seemed to be constantly employed with something. Feeding the child naturally took the most time, and those midnight and early morning calls prevented her from getting more than three or four hours' sleep at a time. It was draining her strength, but she was still shocked when he heard Alex having an argument with Nurse Hani in the room which had been designated the nursery.

" – and I say the child could be bottle-fed," he was saying grimly. He spoke in Greek, but Charlotte was able to understand him.

"If Mrs. Faulkner can only feed him for three or four weeks, it will serve the purpose," Nurse Hani insisted quietly. "There is no substitute for – "

"Don't tell me – mother's milk!" Alex interrupted her

shortly. "I don't believe it. Tests have proved that in some cases, bottle-fed babies are healthier!"

"I was not going to say 'mother's milk'," replied the nurse, steadily. "There is no substitute for the sense of protection the baby receives in his mother's arms. It has also been proved that breast-fed babies are better adjusted children generally."

Charlotte didn't wait to hear any more. Breathing chokingly she went down the steps into the hall and stood trying to calm herself. Of course Alex would want the baby to be bottle-fed. So long as she was feeding him, her presence here was ensured, and Alex would not want that. Not now he had got what he wanted. But why couldn't he have said something to her – not the nurse!

The next time Nurse Hani brought the baby to her to be fed, Charlotte took him reluctantly, and as she unbuttoned her dress, she said: "Don't you think we could start putting him on to the bottle, nurse?"

Nurse Hani made an impatient sound. "Has your husband been talking to you, Mrs. Faulkner?"

"No." Charlotte could speak truthfully. "Why?"

"He has said much the same thing to me. Very well, if that's what you both want. The child is sixteen days old. I don't suppose it will do him any harm."

Charlotte felt the tears pricking at her eyes as she looked at the contented expression on her son's face. His small fist was balled against her breast, his eyes half closed as he eagerly took the milk from her. It was true, she was feeling rather weary, but she would miss these occasions. At moments like these she could almost convince herself that he could not do without her.

The child took easily to the bottle, and it mean that Charlotte could get a good night's sleep. Nurse Hani dealt with the night-time feeding, and gradually he began to sleep for longer periods.

And still Charlotte had had no conversation with Alex

other than of a very lightweight variety. George had arrived a few days ago, and since his arrival, she had seen little of her husband. And then two days before Nurse Hani was due to leave, another young woman arrived. Her name was Glenda Francis, and she was English, and Charlotte was horrified when Alex introduced her as the new nanny. *A nanny!* It seemed to confirm her belief that gradually Alex was making her presence on the island unnecessary.

But what about her? What about her feelings? Not least for the child? There had been no discussion as to what he was to be called, so far as she knew he had not even been registered. Her part in the affair seemed to be over, and slowly but surely she was being manoeuvred into the background. Part of her wanted to rebel, wanted to insist on staying on the island, at least until the child was a few months old. But reason told her that this was foolish. The longer she stayed, the harder it would be to leave. Already she was convinced that the baby recognized her, and once he had started sitting up and taking notice . . .

She paced restlessly about the bedroom, torn by emotions she had not known she possessed. To think she had spoken so carelessly of leaving after the baby was born, to think she had actually wanted to get away!

With a determination born of desperation, she went to see Alex. She found him in the library. George was with him, but he rose at her entrance, and after a brief word of welcome left them. Charlotte's eyes strayed uneasily across the table where they had been working, and suddenly her attention was caught by a legal document pushed carelessly to one side. It was a copy of the contract Mr. Falstaff had given to her, and weakness strengthened into indignation.

"What are you doing?" she demanded. "Drawing up the final agreement? The clause which releases me from this contract? What has George to do with it? Do you discuss it with him?"

Alex was on his feet, his mouth a thin line. "George

is a lawyer," he told her quietly. "I thought you knew that."

Charlotte's lips parted. "You mean – he drew up the contract in the first place? He knows all about it?"

"Yes." Alex inclined his head. "He's the only one who does."

"Oh, indeed!" Charlotte pressed her lips together.

"What do you want, Charlotte? I want to get these papers drawn up. I want to be free of business matters for at least four weeks."

"Why?" Charlotte stared at him. "Is that how long it takes to get a divorce these days?"

"A divorce?" Alex came round the table towards her. "What are you talking about?"

Charlotte backed away. "Divorce! Our divorce! Don't pretend you don't remember, not with that – that contract in front of you!"

Alex looked a little paler under his tan. "You – want a divorce?" he murmured disbelievingly.

"You do."

Alex's eyes narrowed, and then with an exclamation, he snatched her against him, pressing her hungrily along the length of his body. "Does this feel as though I want a divorce?" he demanded thickly. "Dear God, Charlotte, I've tried to keep away from you, to control my feelings, but you try me too far!"

His mouth smothered any protest she might have made, and the passion of his kisses drowned her resistance. He was kissing her deeply and searchingly, seeming to draw the very heart out of her, and she clung to him desperately, unable at the last to let him go.

"Well?" he said, resting his forehead against hers. "Do you still want to leave?"

She moved her head helplessly. "You don't want me to go?"

"No, I don't want you to go. I love you, Charlotte. I've

loved you for a very long time. Long before you even knew I existed."

Charlotte frowned. "You mean – "

"I mean I married you because I loved you, because I wanted to look after you, because I couldn't bear the thought of you alone and lonely, possibly finding someone else before I could tell you how I felt."

Charlotte couldn't take this in. "You mean – you would have married me anyway?" She broke off. "What about those tests?"

"I didn't even check the results. They were purely to convince you I meant what I said.

"But – but why didn't you tell me how you felt? My father – "

Alex shook his head. "Would you have taken me seriously? A man of my age?"

"I might have done."

"I couldn't take the risk. Besides, I didn't have to."

"Did my father know?"

Alex pushed her gently away from him. "I knew we'd come to that!"

Charlotte frowned. "Alex, what happened eight years ago?"

Alex scowled. "What do you know about eight years ago?"

"Nothing. That's why I'm asking you. Oh, George said something . . ."

"George!" Alex looked grim. "I might have guessed."

"Why shouldn't I be told, if it involves me?"

"It doesn't involve you. At least only indirectly."

"Oh, Alex!"

He came towards her, lifting her chin with his fingers, and looking deeply into her eyes. "Answer me something, do you love me?"

Charlotte swallowed, and then nodded her head. "You must know I do."

Alex looked well pleased with her answer. "So – will you

accept that whatever happened eight years ago, we love one another? Our life together is only just beginning. That's why I'm making these arrangements. Why I want at least four weeks of freedom. I want to take you away – somewhere where we can be alone together. Where I can show you that my love for you supersedes everything – even my not inconsiderable affection for our son." He shook his head. "The contract is null and void. It wants destroying. I admit, I used it to get what I wanted. I can be ruthless on occasion, as you'll probably agree. But my motives were not entirely selfish."

Charlotte took deep breath. "But you – you said you had doubts about coming back here after – after – "

"I know I did. It was the truth. Charlotte, whatever you may have expected, I wanted you to settle down on the island, I wanted us to get to know one another. Taking my wife by force was not part of my plan. But you were so – " He broke off. "Can't you imagine how I felt? Particularly after the way you sent me away. I didn't know if I came back that you might not be forced into doing something desperate. You must admit, you were frightened of me."

"To begin with," she murmured, touching his hand. "And then afterwards, I was afraid of myself."

"I knew that," he said gently. "But I still couldn't be sure how you really felt. It was only when I came back this time, when you responded to me of your own volition that I knew – or at least, hoped . . ."

Charlotte passed a confused hand over her eyes. "But what did you mean about loving from me – before I knew of your existence? I never heard – my father mention your name."

"No." Alex's hand fell to his side. "I don't suppose you did." He paused. "Charlotte, you were twelve when I saw you for the first time. A skinny slip of a schoolgirl, with chunky pigtails, dragging around after a man who should have known better than that."

Charlotte's eyes darkened. "Please – don't speak of my father in that way."

"All right, all right." Alex controlled his patience with an effort. "I was what – what? – thirty-three at the time. For ten years I had been running the Faulkner organization. I guess I was cynical and embittered. But I knew you weren't happy."

"My mother hadn't long been dead," Charlotte defended herself. "Daddy and I were both unhappy about that."

"Were you?" Alex bit off the words. "Okay, I'll accept that. Well, I guess I began by feeling sorry for you. But as you grew older, my feelings changed. But you were still much too young. You still are. But God help me, I'm a man, not a saint! And I wanted you. I still do."

"But there were other women?" she ventured.

"Passing affairs," he said indifferently. "Nothing more."

"And – and what about Irena?"

"Irena?" For a minute Alex looked puzzled, then he gave a rueful smile. "Oh, hell, Irena! You surely didn't think I was interested in her?"

"You danced with her. You let her flirt with you."

"I know it. And you were jealous." He put a finger over her lips when she would have protested. "Objective accomplished. Mmm?"

"You mean ..." Charlotte pushed his finger away. "Oh, Alex!"

His eyes softened miraculously. "Well? So now the complication of the baby is out of the way, what is your answer?"

"Do you realize he hasn't even got a name?" she exclaimed, playing for time.

"Provisionally, he's Nicholas Alexander," replied Alex calmly. "Unless you have any other preferences."

"Nicholas Alexander?" Charlotte echoed the names softly. "Oh, no, I have no other preference. I think those names are just ideal!"

"Good. I hoped you would. Well?"

Charlotte knew the moment of truth had come. "You're asking me to take you on trust. To forget about my father's death – his probable suicide – and love you in spite of it?"

she said quietly.

Alex inclined his head. "No easy decision?"

Charlotte made a futile little gesture. "It shouldn't be. An easy decision, I mean. But – " She looked up at him, her heart in her eyes. "Alex, it's no use. I can't leave you. I love you too much."

"Oh, Charlotte!"

His ejaculation was stifled in the silky mass of her hair as he hauled her close against him, burying his face in her neck. To her amazement, she found that he was trembling, and realized with an overpowering feeling of love for him that he had been afraid of what her answer might be. But no matter what self-recrimination she might feel, she knew this was where she belonged, and she prayed her father would understand, wherever he was.

They neither of them heard the knock at the door, and George entered to find them in each other's arms. He cleared his throat rather noisily, and with reluctance Alex broke away from his wife.

"What is it?" he demanded, his impatience evident.

"Vittorio is here. You asked him to come and make the arrangements for taking Nurse Hani back to the mainland."

"Hell, yes." Alex raked a hand through his hair. "I'd forgotten about that." He moved regretfully away from Charlotte. "Wait for me here," he asked her huskily, and she nodded. "I shan't be long."

When the door had closed behind him, George indicated a chair. "Won't you sit down?"

Charlotte subsided into it rather thankfully. Her legs felt none too steady, a combination of her weakness and Alex's lovemaking.

"I gather you're staying," George added gently. "I'm glad."

Charlotte lifted her shoulders and let them fall again. "I love him," she said simply.

"And you can have no doubt now that he loves you,"

remarked George vehemently. "My God, when I think of all these months when he could have told you and didn't. Just to protect your father's memory! I told him he was a fool!"

Charlotte stiffened. It was apparent that George thought Alex had told her everything. But what did everything consist of? She would not have been human if she had not prompted him to go on.

"You – you didn't feel it was necessary, then?" she murmured ambiguously.

"No." George strode across to the windows. "Mortimer is dead – whether by his own hand or not is not important. Why should he be allowed to go on influencing the living?"

"He – he was my father," Charlotte felt bound to say.

"And what about your mother? Doesn't she deserve your pity?"

Fortunately George was not looking at her at that moment, or he could not have failed to notice the look of anguish which crossed her face. "My – mother?" she ventured.

"Yes. Good God, now that you know it was your father's selfishness which caused her heart attack! Don't you have any pity for her?"

Charlotte could not absorb this. "I – I – you think that?"

"I don't think, I –" George suddenly realized what she had said and turned to face her incredulously. "Oh *God!* He didn't tell you, did he? You've let me go on and you know nothing about it, do you? *Alex!* Alex, you idiot!"

"No, please – " Charlotte got to her feet, holding out a hand towards him. "Please, don't be angry with me! But I couldn't help being curious."

"You mean – you mean – you were prepared to live with Alex without knowing the truth?"

Charlotte nodded. "If there is something I don't know, then, yes. Yes, I was."

George shook his head disbelievingly. "Alex said you would. He said you had no need to be hurt any more. And oh, God! Now I've ruined everything."

Charlotte twisted her hands together. "George, you weren't to know. It was as much my fault as yours. You see, I'm not such a blameless character, after all. And – and now you've started, you must go on."

George bent his head, sighing heavily. "How can I?"

"How can you not? Please, George. How did my father cause my mother's heart attack? I – I have to know."

George expelled his breath noisily. "I suppose I must tell you. But if ever Alex finds out . . ."

"He won't. Not yet, at any rate. Please – go on."

George spread his hands in a typically continental gesture. "Very well. Your father was, whether you believe it or not, a compulsive gambler. Nowadays, it's recognized as being as much a disease as drug addiction or alcoholism. But eight years ago it was treated almost lightly. Men gambled and thought nothing of it. Your father was one of them."

"And my mother?"

"Eight years ago, your father lost everything – his house, his business, everything. That was when Alex first became involved. Years ago, your grandfather had done some business with the Faulker organisation. On the strength of that, your father came to us for a loan. At first, Alex refused. Why not? First and foremost, Alex is a businessman. Your father had no securities, no collateral. But eventually he relented, and granted your father the loan. Unfortunately, so far as your mother was concerned, it was too late. She had discovered her husband's debts, and you know what happened."

"Oh, no!" Charlotte felt chilled.

"I'm afraid so. Anyway, the loan went through. Your father spun such a tale about his young daughter, how she would have to leave school and so on. Alex agreed to lend him the money providing he gave up his gambling."

"But he didn't?"

"No. Alex saw him in Cannes, in Monte Carlo, in St. Moritz. Wherever there were casinos, your father could be found. It was obvious that he was mortgaging properties which did not in fact belong to him. The inevitable happened. Your father was a loser, Charlotte. He was flat broke for the second time in his life, and his debts were colossal. So he came crawling back to Alex. Can you imagine how Alex felt! Can you? By this time he knew all about you, had seen you, had begun to care what happened to you. That was when the contract was agreed – an infamous contract indeed, but hardly Alex's fault. He simply wanted to protect you, and there was no other way he could do it. He didn't want to adopt you. That wasn't at all how he felt about you. And anything else would have been open to speculation of the most unpleasant kind. But in the end, your father could not go through with it, apparently. No one will ever really know. Except that that insurance policy stands as witness."

"But how could they let him take out a policy in his financial circumstances?"

"What circumstances? Oh, Charlotte, your father knew what he was doing when he came to Alex. Alex had all the agreements for the loans drawn up privately. No one in the city knew that he owned Mortimer Securities. Mortimer *Securities*!" He gave a short laugh. "What a misnomer that was!"

Charlotte sank down into her chair again. To think that all these months she had blamed Alex for her father's death. As George said, he should have told her.

And yet should he? If she had insisted on knowing the truth before committing herself to him, he might always have wondered whether she had done it out of love – or gratitude. As it was, she was glad she knew the truth, but she was even gladder that she had taken Alex on trust, for the man he was.

The door opened again, and Alex came back into the library. "Okay," he said. "He's waiting to have a word with you, George."

George nodded, and left the room, and after the door had closed, Alex looked quizzically at Charlotte. "Well?" he said. "Have you had second thoughts?"

Charlotte nodded. "And third and fourth ones," she answered, flinging herself out of the chair and into his arms. "Oh, Alex! I'll do my best to make you happy!" She pressed her face against his chest, loving the feel of hard muscle beneath her cheek.

"Hey?" Alex looked tenderly down at her. "What did I do to deserve this?"

Charlotte sniffed, blinking away unexpected tears. "Oh, nothing!" She pressed a kiss against his throat. "Just tell me one more thing – why did you want me to stop feeding Nicholas?" The baby's name sounded enchanting to her ears.

Alex frowned. "Who told you I did?"

"I didn't have to be told. I overheard you and Nurse Hani talking."

"In Greek?"

Charlotte's eyes twinkled. "I haven't been entirely idle while you've been away. Now stop prevaricating. Why did you?"

Alex chuckled. "I could say I was jealous, but I won't," he murmured, amused at her deepening colour. "Honey, how could I get you to myself if you were all tied up here? Besides, you were wearing yourself out, and I was worried about you."

"And Miss Francis?"

"Do you like her?"

"I hardly know her. She seems efficient."

"She has excellent references," agreed Alex seriously. "She was nanny to the children of a business colleague. I wouldn't consider leaving our son in just anybody's hands. But if you're not happy . . ."

"Oh, I am." Charlotte breathed a sigh of contentment. "Why didn't you tell me sooner?"

Alex shook his head. "I guess – I was afraid. Honey, you might still have been hating me, and I don't think I could have borne that."

Charlotte pressed herself against him, feeling his instant response. How much she loved this man who was her husband! To imagine life without him now did not bear thinking about.

"Well, anyway," she breathed huskily, "I'm glad the waiting time is over."

"So am I," answered Alex fervently, against her ear. "I was getting a little tired of sleeping in the dressing room."

Charlotte smiled, putting her hand behind his head and pulling his mouth down to hers. One day she would tell him what George had told her. But not yet. For now it was enough that they had each other, and their son would share the love of both parents. The legend had fulfilled its promise.

Great value in Reading!
Use the handy order form

izabeth Hoy
are the Wild Heart
992)
e Faithless One
1104)
More than Dreams
1286)

umelia Lane
use of the Winds
1262)
Summer to Love
1280)
a of Zanj (#1338)

argaret Malcolm
e Master of
rmanhurst (#1028)
e Man in Homespun
1140)
adowsweet (#1164)

yce Dingwell #2
e Timber Man (#917)
oject Sweetheart
964)
eenfingers Farm
999)

arjorie Norell
rse Madeline of Eden
ove (#962)
ank You, Nurse
nway (#1097)
e Marriage of Doctor
yle (#1177)

ne Durham
v Doctor at
rthmoor (#1242)
rse Sally's Last
ance (#1281)
nn of the Medical
ng (#1313)

Henrietta Reid
Reluctant Masquerade (#1380)
Hunter's Moon (#1430)
The Black Delaney (#1460)

Lucy Gillen
The Silver Fishes (#1408)
Heir to Glen Ghyll (#1450)
The Girl at Smuggler's Rest (#1533)

Anne Hampson #2
When the Bough Breaks (#1491)
Love Hath an Island (#1522)
Stars of Spring (#1551)

Essie Summers #4
No Legacy for Lindsay (#957)
No Orchids by Request (#982)
Sweet Are the Ways (#1015)

Mary Burchell #3
The Other Linding Girl (#1431)
Girl with a Challenge (#1455)
My Sister Celia (#1474)

Susan Barrie #2
Return to Tremarth (#1359)
Night of the Singing Birds (#1428)
Bride in Waiting (#1526)

Violet Winspear #4
Desert Doctor (#921)
The Viking Stranger (#1080)
The Tower of the Captive (#1111)

Essie Summers #5
Heir to Windrush Hill (#1055)
Rosalind Comes Home (#1283)
Revolt — and Virginia (#1348)

Doris E. Smith
To Sing Me Home (#1427)
Seven of Magpies (#1454)
Dear Deceiver (#1599)

Katrina Britt
Healer of Hearts (#1393)
The Fabulous Island (#1490)
A Spray of Edelweiss (#1626)

Betty Neels #2
Sister Peters in Amsterdam (#1361)
Nurse in Holland (#1385)
Blow Hot — Blow Cold (#1409)

Amanda Doyle #2
The Girl for Gillgong (#1351)
The Year at Yattabilla (#1448)
Kookaburra Dawn (#1562)